RIVERDALE

THE MAPLE MURDERS

D0029904

RIVERDALE

THE MAPLE MURDERS

An original novel by Micol Ostow

SCHOLASTIC INC.

Copyright © 2019 by Archie Comic Publications, Inc.

Photos ©: 12 leaf: Benton Frizer/Shutterstock.

ISBN 978-1-338-55262-1

10 9 8 7 6 5 4 3 2 1   19 20 21 22 23

Printed in the U.S.A. 23

First printing 2019

Book design by Jessica Meltzer

PROLOGUE

JUGHEAD

Riverdale: our town. Loosely translated, it means "the valley by the river," and indeed, our town rests against the snaking, rushing path of the Sweetwater, carrying on its rapids the sharp, sticky runoff of maple-tapping season.

Another thing the river carries? Secrets.

If there was one thing we had learned since Jason Blossom first vanished, it's that Sweetwater River has known a lifetime of secrets.

Several lifetimes, to be precise.

Our town was officially established seventy-five years ago, but as the founding families know, it was settled long before then. Our land holds centuries of legacy within its soil—much of it, we were slowly coming to realize, fetid and damning. The sinister secrets and bloodstained pages of our history books date as far back as the very first settlers themselves: from the Hatfield and McCoy–esque feuding of the Coopers and the Blossoms—cousin shooting cousin, brother with his own brother's blood on his hands—to the decimation of indigenous people.

Our town knows darkness, violence, and plague. Most of it brought by its own population. By *people*. If you'd still call them that, knowing all that's finally begun to come to light.

We were learning, we children of Riverdale, that echoes remain. From Jason Blossom's murder (only one of the most recent manifestations of what could reasonably be called a curse upon their house) to the Black Hood, a serial killer stalking sinners.

More recently: a local institution with a thorny past where more than a few of our very own classmates had once been imprisoned and forced to endure traumatic forms of so-called therapy. Gryphons and Gargoyles, an addictive role-playing game that preyed upon its players, driving many to compulsive self-destruction. And a newcomer with a promise of welcoming and acceptance, with a farm he presented as a sanctuary, had a following whose purposes were deeply unclear and wholly suspicious.

All these cryptic and multithreaded dynamics wove back to the town's earliest days, becoming the cornerstones on which our town was built. On which our folklore, our history, sprouted, twisting and coiling like a cluster of vines. Rotting foundations and shaky fault lines—*that* was the Riverdale we were coming to know.

Our shadowy history comes to us in slow-burn revelations: that the modern-day rivalry between the Blossoms and the

Coopers stems from a violent and deadly feud that pitted brother against brother. And the warring factions still yearn for—still *demand*—blood, to this day.

That Barnabas B. Blossom massacred four hundred native Uktena natives to secure his own empire. That the native people have been forced to endure the violence and humiliation of defeat and displacement, not to mention the ongoing pain of near-total cultural whitewashing and a denial of their own collective birthright.

These are the truths that have been revealed, layer by layer.

And if the truths are hardly believable, if they sound more like legend to the casual historian? Well, the legends themselves seep even deeper, into the soil of our town, into our very bones.

The Sugarman, for example: Cheryl Blossom thought he was a boogeyman, a demon fabricated by none other than her own mother, to keep her and her brother afraid and in line. *"Behave, or the Sugarman will whisk you away."*

Little did she know that even the darkest of fairy tales are rooted in some semblance of truth. That the Sugarman wasn't one man but many, an endless continuum. That he wasn't—they weren't—a fairy-tale ogre but criminals.

Criminals who worked for her father.

Another campfire specialty: the Maple Man. A cautionary tale of a beast in the proverbial jungle. The Sugarman would steal you off, abduct you for sinister purposes. But the Maple Man? The Maple Man would devour you whole.

Some dismissed the story as pure urban legend. Some took it as a variation of the Sugarman fable itself—what is maple, after all, if not another form of sugar? But many of us—in fact, I'd venture, most of us—hadn't even heard of the Maple Man. Not until the festival. Somehow, that slice of our town's spoken heritage remained shrouded in a veil of obscurity, skipping an entire generation of Riverdale youth.

But all of us were learning: Though fairy tales themselves may not be real, the wolf is nonetheless always at the door. It wasn't a metaphor.

Not in Riverdale. *Especially* not in Riverdale.

In our town, there is always an ugly truth lurking beneath the lie.

Now, with Archie Andrews's latest brush with danger finally fading (ever so slightly) in our collective mental rearview mirror, all of us—Archie, Betty, Veronica, and me—wanted life to be "normal," or some semblance thereof. We wanted the life that Riverdale's history books, its lauded oral traditions, had promised to us. Maple syrup on Sunday mornings and milk shakes at Pop's after school.

It wasn't just the four of us, either. Normalcy was something every student at Riverdale High craved. Normalcy, and a respite from our realities: that our parents could turn on us, whether it was to disown us, to commit us, to betray us, to abandon us . . . or to disappoint us, yet again. That our teachers and others who were charged to protect us were, on occasion, the most vile predators of all. That evil was a many-headed hydra, and that the idea of triumph was more fantastic than the origins of the mythological beast itself.

Triumph, safety, security—we knew this would never happen, *could* never happen. Our town's past and present were hopelessly tangled in a messy web that would give us no peace in our lifetime.

But still: We hoped. We held it out, a glimmer of optimism. That we could somehow, someday, find our way back to the promise of what Riverdale had intended to be. Riverdale's history wasn't *all* stained and sordid. Our town knew pain, yes: We were learning this over and over again, as our innocence unraveled in the distance.

But Riverdale also knew revelry.

And some of us—those, perhaps, who were familiar enough with the darkness to have made their homes within that waking nightmare—were determined to find our way back to it.

No matter what the cost.

PART ONE: REVELRY

MONDAY

The Riverdale Revels
🍁 OFFICIAL SCHEDULE OF EVENTS 🍁

Monday, 6:00–6:30 p.m.:
Time Capsule Opening, *Pickens Park pagoda*
*After-party to follow at *La Bonne Nuit*.

Tuesday, 5:00–6:00 p.m.:
Riverdale Pet Parade, *Riverdale Elementary*
*Please be sure pets are registered with the front office.
  Leashes required!

Wednesday, 4:00–6:00 p.m.:
Bingo Night, *Riverdale Senior Citizen Center*
*Refreshments will be provided.

Thursday, 6:00–7:30 p.m.:
Motorcade and Music
*Musical performance by Josie McCoy to begin at 6:00 p.m.,
  Town Hall steps.

*Motorcade to depart at 6:15 p.m. promptly, *Town Hall. Procession
  circles down Main Street to the town limits, and back.*

*Enjoy more music, and refreshments courtesy of the Farm after
  the motorcade, *Town Hall lawn*.

Friday, 7:30–9:30 p.m.:
Revels Cocktails and Canapés, *Town Hall*
*Dress your best—cocktail attire is recommended.

Saturday, 10:00 a.m.–6:00 p.m.:
Riverdale Revels Block Party, *Main Street*
*Featuring raffles, prizes, and giveaways from our sponsors, including Andrews Construction, Lodge Enterprises, La Bonne Nuit, WRIV, the *Riverdale Record*, and more!

*Pop Tate's hamburger-eating contest at the Pop's pop-up booth, 12:00 p.m.

*Maple product samples, including syrup, candy, and baked goods, available from Blossom Maple Farms, while supplies last.

*"Go fish" in our maple-pond kiddie pool for a chance to win a home-detailing kit from Mantles' Auto!

*Face painting, pony rides, and a bounce house for our littlest neighbors.

*Bobbing for apples for all ages.

*Take aim at your very own Principal Weatherbee with a delicious maple whipped cream pie (restricted to three throws per person).

*FREE giveaway: retro-style Pop's Chock'Lit Shoppe T-shirts available (one per customer), while supplies last.

Saturday, 7:00 p.m.:
The Royal Maple Pageant and Dance
*Pageant will be held in the *Riverdale High School auditorium*.

*Dance to follow in the gymnasium immediately after crowning.

*Tickets required.

CHAPTER ONE

FP Jones:

So we're a go to announce the Revels at the school today?

Hermione Lodge:

I'm en route as we speak.

FP Jones:

Gotta say, Penelope wasn't thrilled to hear about the tradition coming back. And she wasn't the only one.

Hermione Lodge:

The day I worry about what Penelope Blossom thinks is the day I voluntarily remove myself from office.

Hermione Lodge:

You know the drill—the time capsule was meant to be opened at Riverdale's Jubilee. We may have missed that boat, but nonetheless, I think the timing is perfect to resurrect a happy tradition of CELEBRATING our town. And not one person on the town council could give me a good reason why we shouldn't.

〰〰〰

CHERYL

"Oh, *j'adore!*" I clapped my hands together, jubilant. "The Riverdale Revels! The Royal Maple pageant! What a delightfully OTT festivity we have in store, my darling TeeTee."

It was Monday morning, and we were poised, waiting outside the school auditorium, clustered among throngs of anxious Riverdale High students, all as eager as we were to learn more about the Riverdale Revels. Principal Weatherbee had announced this assembly in an email blast late last night, and we'd all been abuzz with wonder ever since.

I could have done without the various and sundry sweaty elbows in my ribs, but I wasn't exaggerating to Toni; I was absolutely *dying* to hear more about the Revels—such a fun interlude in our oh-so-quaintly small-town lives—and therefore, willing to be more patient and tolerant of the proles than usual.

Toni, however, seemed less than convinced. She tilted her head and gave me some spectacular side eye. "I hear you, Cher," she said. "Revels sounds like a good thing, sure. But—a pageant?"

I watched her face while she considered it, obviously not enthused. She's not really one for pageantry, literally or figuratively (opposites attract, after all).

"Don't get me wrong; I'm in for all the other stuff—a burger-eating contest? Fun times. Pie throwing? Sign me up. But seriously . . . a pageant?" She looked at me, askance.

"I know, I know, it doesn't sound particularly empowered." I bit my lip, tasting Chanel Rouge Allure. "But Weatherbee specifically said it's gender inclusive, which fits perfectly within the mission of our new LGBTQIA group, *n'est-ce pas?* Promise me you'll at least listen with a truly open mind."

I felt a squeeze on my forearm.

"Whose mind is closed? That's a travesty. Did you hear that supposedly it used to be called the Miss Maple pageant? But they updated the name to the Royal Maple to match the pageant's new 'all teens welcome' direction."

It was Kevin Keller, bright eyed as ever, looking every bit the earnest and stalwart do-gooder in his RROTC uniform. I gave him a look and pulled my arm from his grip.

"Careful, please. My skin is not only as pale as fine porcelain, dear Kevin—it's equally fragile. I bruise easily." The curse of being a titian redhead for the ages.

He rolled his eyes. "Of course. Sorry. There, there." He patted my arm—softly this time. "But how fun, right? Quote-unquote 'gender inclusive'"—he actually said *quote-unquote* as he made the gesture with curled fingers—"and I am *all in*."

I smiled. His enthusiasm would have been infectious even if I hadn't already been all in myself. "Likewise, *mon ami*. Now all we have to do is get this ravishing creature on board with us." I gestured to Toni, who still wore that coy expression of strained-but-bemused tolerance. (I knew that look well.) "Frankly, I'm so determined to ensure her participation that I'd give up my own chance to compete in order to throw my full support and attention behind this goddess.

"You're already my queen," I told Toni. "It's time the rest of the town recognized you as the royalty I know you to be."

Kevin looked genuinely shocked to hear that anyone would need persuading to participate in a pageant of any kind. (It was refreshing to have at least one like mind around.)

"Wait, Toni—you're not sold? But your dancing is *on point*—you'd have the talent portion totally sewn up. And obvi, you're beyond gorg." Now he seemed to reconsider. "Actually, I probably shouldn't try so hard to convince you to sign up. Not if I'm hoping to take first prize."

"Convince her? Do we have another conscientious objector in our midst?" It was Veronica herself, resplendent (I could admit, albeit reluctantly) in a black, lace-trimmed A-line dress that would have looked better in red, and on me. (Beauty is truth and truth, beauty, after all.)

"I don't care how inclusive this thing is going to be; it still feels like a throwback to Neanderthal days, if you ask me." Veronica was on a veritable warpath. And over something so silly.

"So you're saying you *wouldn't* want to see Archie take his turn in the spotlight during the swimsuit portion?" Kevin teased.

"Dude, that is *so* not happening." Archie came up behind Veronica and kissed her on the cheek. "Sorry to disappoint you."

"Oh, my Archiekins," Veronica said, smiling at him. "Always such a heartbreaker."

"There's not going to be a swimsuit portion." It was Betty, at Veronica's and Archie's heels, *quelle surprise*, blond ponytail bobbing, a flurry of dove-gray and millennial-pink cashmere. She turned to her hobo of a boyfriend, Jughead. "Wait—is there?"

Jughead shrugged. "No one knows anything about this so-called tradition. It's all more of a rumor at this point."

"A pageant is bad enough, but a swimsuit portion? I will not stand for the objectification," Veronica said. "I'll bypass conscientious objection and fast-forward straight to full-on protest."

"Uh, I might have to start an opposing picket line, in that case." It was Reggie, on cue, leering only semiteasingly.

I held a hand up to dismiss him, focusing my attention on Veronica. "A valiant thought, Norma Rae," I said. "But I think we're getting ahead of ourselves. As I told Toni, I think it behooves us to keep an open mind. I, for one, want to know more about these Riverdale Revels. Why don't we have a seat and hear what our esteemed principal has to say?"

The air in the auditorium was thick and humid, and the seats were packed to capacity. My Vixens had saved seats for Toni and me in the front row, of course (location, location, location), so at least we had the benefit of some leg room in all the chaos and squalor.

Archie, Veronica, and Reggie were a few rows behind us, and from the corner of my eye I saw Betty and Jughead sidle along the edges of the stage, grabbing seats to the right of Weatherbee's podium. Always so stealthy, those two—even when there was nothing particularly untoward underway. Betty had a look of extreme consternation on her face. I doubted it had anything to do with the lingering question of a swimsuit portion. I reached over and took TeeTee's hand in my own, resting our clasped hands in my lap.

Once everyone was seated and the chatter had mostly subsided to a low, unobtrusive murmur, Principal Weatherbee stepped from the wings of the stage and up to a podium centered before us.

"Good morning," he began, his voice smooth. "Thank you, all, for being here." As if it weren't a command performance. As if we weren't dying to hear more about these so-called Revels.

"By now, you've all most likely read the email about the forthcoming Riverdale Revels, to be held this week, starting tonight and going through the weekend. We realize it's short notice, but the decision to revive this beloved town tradition was only just confirmed as of our most recent Town Hall meeting last night."

"Principal Weatherbee—" It was Betty, rising from her seat and chiming in with urgency. "Why the haste? And can you explain why a tradition you're referring to as 'beloved' is something we've never even heard of?"

Weatherbee gave her a strained smile. "I understand that you have questions, Ms. Cooper." He gazed out at the auditorium. "That you *all* may have questions. Luckily, we have a guest with us this morning who will be happy to tell you all about the Riverdale Revels." He turned toward the wings, gesturing at someone standing just offstage. "Please give a welcoming round of applause to our visitor, Mayor Hermione Lodge."

From somewhere just behind me I heard a derisive snort that could only be Veronica.

Louder than Veronica's breathing, though, was the sound of Mayor Lodge's killer heels as she strode onstage, her thick black hair falling perfectly over her shoulders as she moved.

Mayor Lodge certainly *looked* the part of elected official: poised and calm at the front of the room. She took over the podium from Principal Weatherbee with utmost grace.

"Hello," she started, her voice loud and clear. "Thank you for having me today. And thank you to Principal Weatherbee for making the announcement this morning. And"—her eyebrows rose, as though she were only just remembering something—"to Evelyn Evernever, for her help in launching our revival of the Riverdale Revels. Evelyn was kind enough to volunteer her time to help us create the schedule, and she's to credit for the document you all saw in your emails."

Another disbelieving laugh—this time, Betty.

Everyone's skepticism about the festival was perfectly understandable, of course—I could hardly recall an event in this town's recent history that hadn't been sullied by spontaneous bloodshed. But, I don't know, something inside me clearly yearned for the simplicity of a straightforward celebration. It had been too long since we'd experienced unbridled joy. I, for one, was throwing caution to the wind and choosing to embrace enthusiasm.

"Normally, this is the sort of announcement we'd have made in person, rather than online. But in this case, the plans were only finalized yesterday at the Town Hall meeting, as

Principal Weatherbee just explained. Your parents have already received an email from my office detailing the upcoming Riverdale Revels, and they've seen the same schedule you have. But I'm here to give you a little more context about the history of the Riverdale Revels and why we're bringing them back some three-quarters of a century after they faded from practice.

"As you know, our town was founded in 1941, but the early settlers of what would eventually become Riverdale arrived well before that. And while we've always been a town very steeped in tradition, believe it or not, there *are* a few that slipped off our collective radar for quite some time. The Riverdale Revels are just one of those traditions, and we're so thrilled to be able to celebrate them now.

"When the first settlers arrived in this area in the earliest days of the eighteenth century, they had no sense of how hospitable the banks of the Sweetwater would be. There was no guarantee of prosperity to come. The winters—as you all know well—were brutal, and it was grueling work to cultivate the land beyond Fox Forest into suitable homesteads."

I stifled a yawn, and I heard several others in the less-than-captivated audience do the same. I knew all about this; it was part and parcel of being a Blossom. Riverdale *was* the Blossom family, after all; its history begins with our own. But what of these Revels? Why were they so unheard of? It seemed so unlikely that my own family wouldn't know about it. But then again, all *too* likely that Mumsie knew—but kept it from me, for her own odious, unknowable reasons.

"But these early citizens persevered," Mayor Lodge continued. "After a few successful harvests, they decided to commemorate the occasion with a festival, a celebration of the land's bounty. They rejoiced, and feasted, in what would later be known as"—she took a deep breath for dramatic input—"the Riverdale Revels."

"Points for alliteration, at least," Toni whispered. I squeezed her hand.

"We don't know much about the early Revels. Those chronicles were sparse, and very little concrete information remains. What we do know is that, while Riverdale Revels are a tradition dating back to our first settlers' earliest harvests, before our town was officially founded, the event grew to a longer celebration, sometimes spanning a full week of feasts, concerts, and Town Hall dances."

From the back of the room, I heard Kevin Keller call out, "And a pageant?" The hope in his tremulous voice was simply darling. A few students whooped in response. Clearly Kevin and I weren't the only ones excited for the festivities.

Mayor Lodge must have thought so, too. She smiled. "Yes, the pageant. A later addition to the lineup and an event tailor-made for our Riverdale High students. I'm sure you're all eager to hear more about it." Kevin led the cheers that rose up from the crowd. I snapped politely, unwilling to break the connection with my beloved TeeTee to clap like a commoner.

"At the center of the—well, pun intended, I suppose—revelry was the Miss Maple pageant. Originally, it was a traditional beauty pageant, but of course, with the advent of modern times comes modern ideals. So we're giving Miss Maple our own twist. We've renamed it the Royal Maple pageant, and *all* are welcome to participate. We hope that many of you will."

The buzz from the crowd was building now, as many people starting whispering among themselves, already making plans.

I raised my hand. "Yes, Cheryl," Mayor Lodge acknowledged me.

"Madam Mayor, according to the email, the Revels begins tonight. And the pageant will be held on Saturday—*this* Saturday?"

She nodded coolly. "Correct. Tonight will be our kickoff event: the opening of the Jubilee time capsule."

I waved my hand, still focused on my own issue. "That hardly seems like enough time to perfect our acts. And to find the perfect formal wear!" I protested. Others murmured in agreement around me.

Mayor Lodge smiled. "I appreciate the concern, Cheryl. But I have no doubt you, of all people, will be able to pull something inimitable together in the allotted time."

"Why the rush?" Veronica called, challenging, from behind me. "The Jubilee has come and gone. No one mentioned a time capsule before now. I have to say, it feels a little odd that we're hearing about all this so last-minute. Odd, and maybe . . . suspicious."

The mayor took a deep breath, clearly considering her response. "Well, Veronica, I suppose you're not wrong. In fact, in 1941, upon the event of the town's official founding, the town council sealed a time capsule with the explicit intention of its being opened seventy-five years later, during our Jubilee celebration. This was how they honored their very last Riverdale Revels."

"They just canceled their yearly festival?" Betty blurted, glancing first at Jughead and then over at Veronica.

Mayor Lodge tucked her hair behind her ear. "They *evolved*," she said deliberately. "The Revels was a celebration that commemorated a more tenuous, fraught time. Since the town was ushering in what they anticipated to be great vibrancy and less uncertainty, they thought the time capsule was a fitting tribute. Soon, many other traditions would take over. Our midnight New Year's pancake breakfast, for one."

I stood up. I'd had enough. "And while normally I'd say, who doesn't love a piping hotcake, fresh from the griddle, I think it's time to lay off the interrogation mode, classmates. This is a gift festival. Let's not look it in the mouth."

Around me, cheers swelled again. My dour, do-gooder cousin and her rejects-from-a-John-Hughes-open-call cohorts were clearly in the minority with their doubts and aspersions. The rest of us Bulldogs? We were ready to revel.

Mayor Lodge gestured for us to quiet down. Slowly, we did. "Of course, the time capsule was intended to be opened at the 75th Anniversary Jubilee. But, well . . ." She shifted for a moment, seeming to consider something.

She looked out at us, gaze set. "It's no secret that at the time of the Jubilee, Riverdale was having a . . . *rocky* go of it. It was determined that it wasn't the right time to open the time capsule."

"Interesting use of the passive, there," Toni said. I elbowed her.

"Since then, however, the"—she seemed to be grasping for the right phrasing—"the *challenges* we've faced as a town haven't lessened."

"Uh, understatement," someone heckled. The audience laughed, but it was uneasy.

"There has been *plenty* to worry about and to stress over," Mayor Lodge said simply. "And we in Town Hall thought— what better time to take a moment and recapture some of what makes Riverdale special? The founders wanted it this way, and it was our mistake to miss the specific milestone they dictated. But we'll make our own milestone now: It's the right time to bring the Revels back."

"Mayor Lodge, I couldn't agree more," Principal Weatherbee said, stepping up and smoothly taking over the podium once again. "Thank you so much for taking the time to come speak with our students. Students: Let's show our dedicated mayor some gratitude, shall we?"

Dutifully, we applauded.

"There will be tables for signing up for the pageant located outside the cafeteria at lunchtime," Principal Weatherbee went on, "alongside information and volunteer sheets for other events as well. It's all in the welcome-letter packet that was sent to you this morning. We hope you'll all loan your talents to as much of the Revels as possible."

"If you can't make it to the sign-up tables, but you still want to register for the pageant, just see me!" Evelyn Evernever hopped up from her own front-row perch. Her voice rang with energy. There was at least one student Mayor Lodge didn't have to worry about bringing on board with this celebration.

The assembly drawing to a close, I turned back to my TeeTee.

"You've got a look in your eye," she said, assessing me oh-so-accurately. "I recognize it."

"Who, me?" I winked. "I'm just excited for the Revels."

"You really want me to compete so badly that you're willing to sit it out yourself?"

I blushed. "Why, Antoinette, am I that transparent?"

"Okay," she sighed. "I'll do it. You can . . . I don't know, train me or mentor me, or whatever the right wording is for 'guide me in the ways of pageantry.' *If* you're not weird about it."

I squealed. "Oh, *merveilleux*! It will be grand. And it'll be a formidable addition to your college transcript when you emerge victorious." I could see it now: my beloved, onstage, resplendent in a crown and that killer smile of hers. "I do so love an opportunity to be opulent. I promise, I will carve you like a modern-day sapphic Pygmalion."

"No, see—already a little weird. I'm open-minded, but I'm nobody's Eliza Doolittle."

"Of course you're not," I said, kissing her. "Even if you *are* my fair lady."

CHAPTER TWO

Betty:

V, you weren't at lunch. Kevin was asking if you were gonna sign up for the Revels. Evelyn's been at that registration table for three periods now. No idea how she even got out of class.

Veronica:

And students are clamoring to put their names down, I gather?

Betty:

It's not NOT popular. Let's put it that way.

Veronica:

I have some other ways I could put it. Went off-campus for lunch to talk to my mother. Stay tuned.

Betty:

Good luck!

VERONICA

Riverdale's Town Hall, where the mayor's office was located, was nothing short of a small-town architectural gem: soaring ceilings, antique wood polished to a gleam, and cavernous atria—all the better for a dramatic entrance. Which was precisely what I was going for. I stormed into my mother's office, shoving my way past her anxious assistant, heels clacking purposefully on the tiled floor.

"Veronica." My mother gave me a tight smile. "This is a surprise. Shouldn't you be in school . . . where I last saw you?" Everything about her perch behind her desk in her mayoral office was full-on extra: imposing, imperious, and impeccable. Her eyes were intense, boring into me, rimmed by a pair of tortoiseshell Dolce & Gabbana glasses that perfectly played up her prim-but-chic silk Celine blouse.

I waved an arm as I settled into the seat across from her so that we were positioned like two cardsharps on opposite sides of a poker table.

"Fear not, your daughter is no truant," I said. "It's my lunch period, so I thought it would be a good time to pop out to talk to you about this latest . . . *travesty* to be visited on our student body." I drummed my fingers against the desktop, waiting for—I don't know, some sort of defensive explanation.

She raised an eyebrow, offering nothing. So it was going to be like *this*?

"I'm sorry," I said, briefly reconsidering my tact. I swallowed, forcing back bile. "It's possible I'm overreacting." I thought about it again, and my heart rate instantly kicked up a few paces. *No, not overreacting.*

"No, I take it back. I'm definitely, *emphatically* not sorry. Mom . . . *a pageant?*"

Still nothing, not even a microexpression. No wonder she and my father were such skilled negotiators.

"*Pageant,*" I repeated. "Did I accidentally stumble into a late-nineties rom-com? Next thing you're going to tell me we're doing a shopping spree at Riverdale Mall." I shuddered.

My mother finally turned her attention from the giant computer monitor she'd been hiding behind. She sighed.

That sigh gave me pause. I daresay I might have been better off when she was still hiding behind her monitor, playing coy. But no: I was here on a noble mission. And my mother should have known: My steely gaze is every bit as practiced and as formidable as hers. I steadied it at her now, crossing my arms over my chest and awaiting her reply. *Don't blink*, I thought, willing it. It was easier said than done, but I'm no novice when it comes to psychological warfare.

"Don't be silly, Veronica; I know you'd never shop at a *mall*." She smiled at her own joke.

"But yes, *mija*," she went on. "A pageant. I don't understand why you're making such a production out of this. It will be fun! You and your friends might even enjoy it! It's a small, nostalgic part of a bigger celebration."

"It's sexist and archaic." *For starters.* Also: tacky, but TBH that was lower on my list of complaints.

"Oh, come now, Veronica. No one's challenging your . . . sense of female empowerment. You're being too dramatic. It's not like you've never paraded your . . . *assets* onstage before. Need I point out: You're a River Vixen."

"Gloria Steinem called; your betrayal of second-wave feminism is complete," I snapped. The River Vixens weren't tacky; they were tradition. It was completely different on so many levels.

"Mom, it's the twenty-first century. You of all people should know that cheerleading is, at long last, *finally* recognized as a legitimate sport: one which requires training, endurance, and athleticism. Perhaps, yes, once a upon a time, cheerleaders were denigrated as purely ornamental, a decorative backdrop to the masculine pursuit of alpha-male sport. Little more than a halftime show at best. But that's changed. We *compete* now. The Vixens *won* our last tournament. With choreography *I* helped arrange. You know that."

Even understanding how Mom tended to fall in line with my paterfamilias, in the most stereotypically nuclear-family pattern, this stance felt off-brand for my mother, a working-woman who was actively involved in both big business and politics, after all.

She took off her glasses and rubbed at her temples. "Okay, I apologize. I certainly didn't mean to imply anything about your feminist ideals, Veronica. You know I'd never objectify my own daughter."

Of course not. I had to roll my eyes. "Well, there *was* the time you asked me to use my feminine wiles to influence Archie's decisions, if I recall," I reminded her. "Also, when you and Daddy asked me to escort that world–class sleaze Nick St. Clair around Riverdale because you two wanted to be in business with his parents."

I wasn't wrong, but it wasn't what she wanted to hear. None of the Lodges enjoy being put in our places. I could see the flicker of annoyance cross her perfectly chiseled cheekbones.

"Fine," she snapped. "Never say *never*. But this pageant is happening, *mija*. Saturday. Tonight we're kicking off the Riverdale Revels by opening a seventy-five-year-old time capsule in Pickens Park, and you will be by my side with a smile on your face through the whole overblown affair."

"A command performance." I sighed. "Not to mention the after-party at La Bonne Nuit that I found out about via email, at the same time as every other person in this town."

"I *am* sorry about that. And of course, the mayor's office will see to it that you're reimbursed for all expenses."

"And I assume I'm expected to smile through that one, as well?"

"Naturally. Think of what it would look like if the mayor's own daughter didn't join in." Mom tapped her perfectly painted nails against her desk.

"It would look like the mayor's own daughter doesn't believe in festivals that highlight chauvinistic, outdated traditions like beauty pageants. Honestly, it would probably play well with your more progressive constituents."

Mom laughed. "This is Riverdale, Veronica. Progressive or not, my constituents value tradition. It was some of my most progressive constituents themselves who rallied to have the celebration brought back and the time capsule opened."

"I find that hard to believe."

"Maybe you do, *mija*. But I don't need you to believe; I just need you to behave. Right now, this town needs the Revels more than ever. Or should I remind you of how . . . tumultuous things have been even just in the time since we've arrived?"

I shook my head. Of course she didn't need to do that. Since she and I had moved to Riverdale, we'd seen the aftermath of a familial murder, a serial killer who'd terrorized our town (with a copycat or two thrown into the mix for good measure), and some mafioso violence (that *may* or may not have involved the Lodges, ourselves, though I, for one, wasn't talking . . .).

And most recently . . . my own Archiekins victimized by my daddy dearest, Fizzle Rocks on the street, and Gryphons and Gargoyles in back alleys and underground game rooms. All that was only the tip of the proverbial iceberg. *Tumultuous* was beyond an understatement.

"So that's it, then? The pageant is happening."

"The Revels are happening; the pageant is happening; the unveiling and the after-party are happening, tonight." Mom was resolute.

"I hereby reserve the right to say 'I told you so' later, when nothing good whatsoever comes out of all this."

"Your concerns are duly noted."

"But you won't actually *do* anything about them," I countered.

"Correct." She sighed again. If she were the type of woman who had to think about worry lines, I knew this conversation would be contributing to them. But things being as they were, she mostly just adopted an expression more suited to the "before" model in an aspirin ad.

"Because there's nothing *to* do," she went on. "The Revels are another page from Riverdale's history—and it's time to bring them back. Slightly overdue, as a matter of fact, in terms of the time capsule."

She leaned in. "Come, now, Veronica—aren't you even the least bit curious about what's inside? When else can you have such a pure peek into our town's history?"

"Because everything about Riverdale's *history* is so wholesome and pure and worth revisiting." Please. Our town was basically a Lynchian nightmare—with really good milk shakes. Mom knew it as well as anyone. I was here to call her bluff.

Except, apparently, it *wasn't* a bluff, so there was nothing to call. She was not going to back down about this.

"In case you haven't noticed, Veronica, our 'wholesome, pure' town is in a death spiral these days. And I'm the mayor—meaning, it's my job to bring hope and faith back to the people. A fun celebration and a return to our roots will do just that."

I opened my mouth to protest, but she held up a hand, cutting me off.

"And as for your so-called progressive friends, I'm sure even they will embrace the pageant. Your mother is not a dinosaur, *mija*. Rest assured, everyone on the town council and the planning committee has been meeting about this festival for weeks. The idea of making it gender-inclusive was supported unanimously."

"Right. Equal-opportunity objectification," I snarked instinctively. "How woke of you." But some of the bite had drained from my voice. I had to admit, it was a good call. And it would make for an interesting event, if nothing else.

"I'm disappointed in you, Veronica. Here I thought you'd

be so enthusiastic about how subversive our small town is being."

"Even if you *are* taking a hallowed—albeit, forgotten—tradition into the current times," I said, steeling my resolve all over again, "I can all but guarantee you: This festival will be nothing short of a catastrophe."

CHAPTER THREE

KEVIN

"This pageant is going to be *amazing*."

"I still can't *believe* you're so on board with this." Veronica's eyebrows knit together in an evil-queen glare.

"And *I* can't believe you're being such a downer. Veronica Lodge, missing a chance to primp and preen?"

It was late Monday afternoon, and we were in the student lounge for a study period, continuing the ongoing debate about the Royal Maple.

Rather, *Veronica* was continuing the debate about the pageant. Basically, everyone else in the whole school had made their peace with it, either planning to compete or participate in some way, or else just looking forward to the spectacle. (I mean, speaking from the small, anecdotal sample survey conducted by yours truly.)

But not Veronica. Her feelings hadn't cooled with the passing of time. Frankly, it was a buzzkill. I had expected more from my resident fashionista.

"It's *sexist*." She folded her arms, delightfully pouty with her face framed by a lace Peter Pan collar. Sort of a Selena Gomez by way of Blair Waldorf. (But still, somehow, all her own. *How* did this girl not want to strut her stuff in a pageant? It was beyond me, and it was downright criminal.)

"Okay, okay, you did it. You're on record as an objector and the leader of Riverdale's own Mayday resistance. You shall henceforth be known as Elizabeth Cady Stanton Lodge. Done and done. You're making me mix my girl-power metaphors, and it's messy. So"—I smiled, rubbing my hands together—"can we *please* move on? I want to talk *ensembles*. Because there's definitely going to be an evening-wear portion, and I *know* you have tips on how to wear a Marchesa."

Veronica smiled. "Well, I'm not going to argue that. That team can drape—credit where credit is due. And the winter look book is exceptional."

I gasped. "Tell me you got a sneak peek and you never mentioned it!" This was unacceptable. Insult to injury.

"Oh, V, he's never going to let you off the hook now." Betty settled herself on the couch next to Veronica, nursing a coffee in a to-go mug. Jughead hovered behind her, methodically breaking off squares from a chocolate bar and enjoying the show.

"You guys do realize you're basically speaking a foreign language now, right?" Archie asked. He had settled himself over the back of the couch. Veronica reached up and rested a hand on his thigh. "Draping. Look books. I need a translator."

Veronica laughed. "Sorry! I know you're more denim than Dior, Archiekins. And sorry, Kevin! I should have mentioned the look book earlier, I know."

"You *should* have invited me over to peruse it with you," I grumbled, teasing.

"Okay, yes. But to be fair, it didn't come up before we were talking about *evening-wear portions.*"

I shot her a look and she quickly rephrased.

"You're right. What was I thinking? I should have brought it up myself, sans external impetus. There should have been an engraved invitation."

"Yes, there should have. But you're forgiven . . . *if* you agree to get on board so we can do this thing and have a blast, okay?"

She bit her lip. "It *really* doesn't feel like my thing. And honestly, Kev—I don't want to compete against you!"

I thought about it. "Okay, I hear that. And I guess if I were able to pick and choose, I wouldn't necessarily want to compete against you, either. But I still want to do this *with* you! Veronica, who else is going to help me choose the right hair product for the different event segments? Wax versus serum? Tousled versus clean-cut?" I made puppy-dog eyes at her, pleading. I was only half kidding, too.

(Serum, though. Clean-cut. Always. Stick with the classics, that's my thing.)

Maybe it was silly (okay, it was *definitely* silly)—but how many chances was I going to get to be in a pageant? At least here in *Riverdale*, in high school? I've been out and proud for a while now, and everyone has been incredibly cool about it (especially my dad; he's the best).

But Riverdale is not the most forward-thinking environment in the world. I mean, it was just last year that we all learned how the Sisters of Quiet Mercy were running an underground *conversion therapy* program out of their institution. So a gender-inclusive pageant felt like a step in the right direction—and an opportunity for fun not to be missed.

And Veronica Lodge was the obvious partner in crime for such an event. She *had* to understand that.

"Elizabeth Cooper," I prodded, "talk some sense into your girl."

"Kev, I feel you," Betty said, "but V is her own woman. I think that's kind of the root of this whole thing in the first place."

"But *you* guys are going to do it," I asked. "Right?"

"Actually . . ." She trailed off, glancing at Jughead. His interest level in his chocolate bar rocketed to a level that could only be described as *preternatural*.

He caught her staring and swallowed, taking a second to lick his fingers before balling up the wrapper and tossing it in the trash.

"Oh, Kevin, you're barking up the wrong tree," he protested, smiling. "You know full well that if Archie is more denim than Dior, then *I'm* more Hercule Poirot than Hugo

Boss. And Weatherbee already tapped Betty and me to cover the Revels for the *Blue and Gold*. So I don't think we'd have time to do the pageant, even if we *were* so inclined. Which—and I really can't say this enough—I'm definitely not."

"Sorry, Kev," Betty said, looking genuinely regretful.

"We will happily—if at least *semi*-sardonically—cheer you on from the wings," Jughead put in. "Well, speaking for myself. You can probably count on Betty for at least ten percent less cynicism."

"Thirty, minimum," she confirmed.

"Aim for forty. Kevin will need his squad in his corner, full-on, if he truly intends to beat my Antoinette."

We all looked up to see Cheryl Blossom standing, hands on hips, Wonder Woman–style, a challenging arch to her eyebrow.

"What about *you*, Cheryl?" I asked. "You're not worried about going head-to-head with your girlfriend?"

"Oh, I won't be competing myself," Cheryl said with a wave of her hand. The chiffon sleeves of her blouse flowed dramatically as she gesticulated. "After careful consideration, I realized that I've had more than my share of moments in the sun, ever since first being crowned Miss Junior Sweetwater as a young child at the River Run country club." She sighed, deep in her own reverie. "My halcyon salad days."

Jughead smirked. "Those must have been good times."

She scrunched her perfect features in a flash of a scowl. "You wouldn't know, cretin." Then she beamed again. "In any event, if you do participate, please be aware that I will be your mistress of ceremonies for the evening."

"*You're* going to be *emcee*?" Betty asked.

I got it: On the one hand, running the show as resident HBIC was very on-brand for Cheryl. On the other, willfully giving up the chance to be crowned victor was . . . not.

"In point of fact," she said, crisp, "my primary duties will involve acting as Toni's coach and confidante. Being emcee in the actual pageant is the least I can do to show solidarity with my fellow students. Almost everyone has signed up. You folk are—as ever—well behind the curve. Reggie got the whole football team doing it."

"Not me," Archie said. "My dad's gonna be crazy busy building sets and stuff for the Revels, which means I'll be helping him."

"Yeah, and I'm pretty sure Josie said she was bowing out, too, since she's focusing on performing at the Thursday-night event. Motorcade and Music or something?" I put in.

"That's right, Kevin—Motorcade and Music."

It was Evelyn, popping up and penetrating our little bubble even more stealthily than Cheryl had. She was joined by Ethel, both of them clutching overflowing manila file folders. She gave a bright smile that was maybe only two shades away from being manic. It was . . . unnerving.

"Evelyn, hi," I said, trying to be welcoming. I knew Betty had plenty to hold against the girl—Evelyn's father, Edgar

Evernever, was the leader of the Farm, which Betty's mom and sister, Polly, were totally obsessed with—but Evelyn had never been anything but friendly to me.

"Hey, Ethel," Betty said, waving at her. Ethel gave a wave to the group of us. She was much more low-key than Evelyn, but then, that was just her general demeanor overall. "What do you have?"

"These are all the registrants," Evelyn said. "I'm taking them to Weatherbee's office now to be logged. It's a lot," she said, looking meaningfully at Veronica. "So many of your fellow students have signed on."

"What she means is, anyone worthy enough to compete has signed on. Anyone who's anyone," Cheryl said. "And, of course, an assortment of rando wannabees. But that can't be avoided."

"Just think of it as an act of charity," Jughead suggested, arching an eyebrow.

"It's . . . nice that you're so into helping out with the Revels, Evelyn," Betty said. Her voice was low and unreadable.

Evelyn straightened, the movement slightly inscrutable. "Of course. The Farm is just so pleased to have made a home for ourselves here in Riverdale. Why shouldn't we want to celebrate this town and all it has to offer?"

Betty rolled her eyes, but still, even knowing how skeptical she was, how corny she thought the whole thing was—I felt a little charge in my stomach just thinking about it. Celebrate Riverdale? Eh, it depended on the day. But celebrate, in general? *Yes, please.*

"You should know that spots are filling up," Evelyn said. "If you're serious about participating, this might be your last chance."

I held my hands out to Veronica in a namaste. "Pretty please with a promise to binge-watch your fave Shondaland guilty pleasure at our next sleepover, without judgment?"

(It was one of her darker secrets, but Veronica had a deep and unironic love of complete works of Shonda Rhimes, despite how unabashedly OTT we know them to be. Fun fact: She's never missed an episode of *Grey's Anatomy*.)

Veronica narrowed her eyes. "Kevin! That was a to-the-grave secret." She laughed. "The first rule of Shondaland is we don't talk about Shondaland." She sighed. "All right, you've sold me. If you can't beat them, join them."

My heart jumped in my chest. "Does that mean you'll do it?"

"Not *quite*," she said, holding up a hand. "But it means I'll be your coach, if you'll have me."

Coach. *That was maybe even better than Veronica being in the pageant herself.* I'd get the benefit of her unassailable expertise *and* the fun of hanging out with her. (And also, maybe a peep at that Marchesa look book sooner rather than later.)

"Yes, yes, a thousand times yes. I declare myself to be the

willing Kendall to your Kris," I said, solemn. "Mold me in your image."

"Oooh, I sense a rom-com makeover montage in the making," Jughead said, raising an eyebrow. "The only question is, do we set it to 'Pretty Woman,' or 'Sharp Dressed Man'?"

"Wrong." I stood from the sofa and reached for Ethel's file folder. "The *only* question is, where is that registration form?"

Ethel handed me a sheet and pointed to the line where I needed to scribble my name. She passed me a pen. "Excellent choice, Kevin," she said.

"She's right." Evelyn's eyes shone. "It's going to be a real blast. You'll see."

∧∧∧

From: Evernever, Evelyn
To: ALL-FARM LIST: YOUTH
Re: The Royal Maple Pageant

To all high school members of our Farm family:

My father and the rest of our family at the Farm would like to encourage you to participate in the Riverdale Revels, and especially the Royal Maple pageant. Please see me if you'd like to talk further. And sign up for the pageant soon—slots are filling up quickly!

*The final day to sign up is tomorrow, but the sooner you commit, the sooner you can start to prepare! Remember that when you appear onstage, you'll be representing all of your Farm brothers and sisters!

CHAPTER FOUR

Yo, Bulldogs! Evelyn's finalizing the pageant contestants TOMORROW. Anyone sitting it out, be prepared to swim the Fox Forest channel at midnight, naked, every night next month. The Bulldogs are coming out for this one, bros. It's gonna be epic.

Moose:

UGH FINE

Chuck:

Already signed up, bro.

Archie:

No can do. Gotta help my dad. But I'll definitely be there for the show.

Reggie:

Dude, you're the ONLY one with a good excuse! You need to help me kick the other guys' butts, get 'em in line.

Archie:

I'll see what I can do . . .

∿∿∿

Jughead:

Serpents, a few of you have asked if you're supposed to be going to the pageant. Given that my dad's the sheriff, I'm gonna ask you as your king to consider participating. But for myself, I'm gonna tell you, when it comes to the pageant—just follow your heart.

Fangs:

Jug, man—I'm gonna do it.

Sweet Pea:

Me and Toni are in, too. Should be kind of a kick.

Jughead:

Better you than me, Fangs.

Fangs:

Take it you're out?

Jughead:

Ah, believe it or not, I've just been assigned a Revels duty of my own.

Fangs:

?

Jughead:

Oh, no. It'll have to be a surprise. Don't worry, it's a good one.

⌒⌒⌒

BETTY

Dear Diary:

Okay, I'll admit—even if it _does_ feel sort of old-fashioned—I definitely think the Riverdale Revels are going to be fun.

I think.

Is it, I don't know...<u>suspicious</u> that Mayor Lodge is trotting out some long-forgotten tradition <u>now</u>, when our town's been plagued with countless scandals and heartaches? I mean...yeah, maybe a little. But—I don't know...even if she's reviving the Revels for weird or not-great reasons...

Maybe she's <u>right</u>? Maybe we could use a little celebration, a little fun.

At least, that's what I told V while we walked home from school. She was stopping by the speakeasy, and I was going to swing by

Pop's. Juggie wanted a snack, no surprise, but he had some stuff to take care of with the Serpents first.

"It'll be good for us," I said. "Revelry! It's right there in the name of the event. Come on."

It was late fall and we were well into the school year but still waiting on the first real snap in the air. Sweater weather, which I love, and the first few orange-tinged leaves crunching under our feet, but the promise of icy winter nights still far off in the distance. In short, it was my favorite time of year.

"You're too nice, B," Veronica said, shaking her head. Her black cape draped behind her as we walked, giving everything she said an extra layer of drama and foreboding. "Where's my Dark Betty when we need her?"

I gave her a look. "Oh, she's still in there, I promise you. She'll come out when it's time, raring to go. But let's keep her on ice until we're ready for, you know, the big guns." I was slowly but surely starting to get comfortable with my darkness. But boundaries were good, too. I didn't like feeling like I could go off, lose control at any minute and without warning. Hence: ice and boundaries.

"Which clearly implies that you don't think we are yet. Ready for the big guns, that is." I could tell she didn't totally agree.

I sighed. "No, not yet." Our heels made satisfying scraping sounds against the sidewalk as we walked. "I mean, I hear what you're saying—it's been a hot minute since the last time we had a cele-bration or an event in this town that didn't end with literal murder, so, you know: There's definitely a track record. But also: With all the craziness going on literally <u>all the time</u> here, if your mom—<u>the mayor</u>—is telling us to take a second and enjoy, you know, a block party and a silly beauty pageant? Why the hell shouldn't we?"

I grabbed her by the elbow. "Come on. You <u>know</u> prepping for the pageant with Kevin is going to be total fun. It's an event tailor-made for the two of you."

"Your powers of persuasion are not bad," she said. "I must admit, Dark Betty may be useful for some of my more complex plotting and revenge scenarios, but classic Betty is wise beyond her years. <u>Vive le classic Betty</u>. Accept no imitations." She linked her arm through mine.

"Thanks, V. I'm feeling original-flavor Veronica, myself. I guess we just make a perfect team."

∧∧∧

V waved me inside when we got to Pop's—she had to take a quick phone call from a supplier for the speakeasy. "Puff pastries for the after-party were surprisingly difficult to get with mere hours' notice," she explained, rolling her eyes. I laughed and headed in without her.

When I entered the diner, Jughead was already waiting at the counter. He was hunched over a cheeseburger the size of his face. FP sat on the stool beside him, eating a burger of his own. It was like looking into a mirror of Jughead Future, and that made me smile.

Behind the counter, Pop was wiping down glasses and watching Jug eat with a look of affectionate wonder.

(It's a look I know well—I have a version of it of my own.)

"You beat us here?" I asked. I know nothing stands between Jug and a burger, but still—it was impressive.

"Dad gave me a lift on the bike."

"Hey, Betty," FP said, taking a sip of his soda.

"That eager for your after-school snack, huh?" I teased.

"Well, yeah—always. But actually"—he looked at me, and I saw a glint in his eye that was slightly concerning—"turns out, Dad had some news. Which couldn't wait for sharing with you. So it all worked out, in a sense."

"Hmm. 'In a sense'? I'm guessing that depends what I think of the news." I sidled up to the stool beside him and leaned in for a quick kiss. He smelled like boy shampoo and worn leather.

The door chimed again. "Puff pastries are a go," Veronica said, looking at me. "Hello, Joneses, and hello, Pop. Slow day?" She glanced around the diner. It did seem quieter than usual, but I chalked it up to so many people being caught up in prepping for the Revels. Jughead took advantage of the interruption to tuck into his burger.

Veronica stepped behind the counter to fish the diner's ledger out from its shelf to have a another look, I assumed, at the most recent margins. As the newly minted owner of Pop's, she couldn't afford to be optimistic about the business; she had to deal with actual dollars-and-cents reality.

Luckily, she didn't have to worry quite as much about the speakeasy downstairs. La Bonne Nuit was impeccably designed and decorated, and the entertainment was sophisticated and aspirational. It was a place most of my friends from school hadn't even <u>realized</u> was everything they'd never known they wanted. A place to hang that wasn't "just" Pop's, with an air of elegance and a chill, low-key New York City vibe...? Veronica knew what Riverdale needed. And in buying the building back from her endlessly conniving dad, she not only landed herself the hot spot of her dreams—she basically saved Pop's, our local touchstone, one of the beating hearts of our town itself.

But business was still growing, I knew. And now that Veronica had broken free of her father's barbed purse strings, she worried a lot about her ability to be independent, financially and otherwise. She didn't like to talk about it, but I knew. For instance, at that moment I could see it in the way her forehead wrinkled up as she ran her manicured finger across columns, surveying the data. If nothing else, my girl V is <u>definitely</u> resourceful, and ultimately, she's got this—but even if the mayor's office claimed to be covering the cost of the after-party, the speakeasy would end up taking at least a small hit.

An idea occurred to me. "Pop—the burger-eating contest on Saturday sounds like it'll be fun!" I said. "V, maybe La Bonne Nuit could be on hand to provide custom mocktails? Something with ginger, to help with digestion?"

"Betty, that is straight genius," Veronica said. "Normally I'd say the only appropriate accompaniment to a Pop's burger is a milk shake, but in a burger-eating contest, that would probably be overkill. Now, a light, fruity ginger spritzer on the other hand? That could be the perfect palate cleanser. I'll talk to Reggie about experimenting this week. That boy has really proven himself a sophisticated mixologist, I must say."

"Even being partial to my own milk shakes, on this, I'd have to agree," Pop chimed in. "This sounds like a great plan."

"Then it's settled," I said. "Veronica will create a perfect drink for the contest and La Bonne Nuit stays on the tip of everyone's tongues at the Revels. And we all agree I am a certified genius. And in the meantime, Jughead can fill us in on his big news."

Jughead swiveled on his chair. His eyes were practically blazing. I couldn't tell if that was a good thing or a bad thing—but I had an idea. "You'll never guess who's in charge of opening the time capsule tonight."

"What?" I stared at him, incredulous. "You? Why? I mean—" I faltered, realizing how that sounded. "It's not like I don't think you could do it. Clearly you could do a great job. You will do a great job! It just... doesn't exactly sound like the kind of thing you'd normally be up for."

I actually kind of loved the idea, already imagining Juggie up on that pagoda, sporting that unique mix of startled disaffection he wore so well.

"Well, yeah—it's definitely not. I mean, it's basically anathema to me. In my soul I'm sort of fundamentally opposed to everything the Revels represent in the first place. And to be, like, part of it? Yeah, super not my thing. You could say that. You know me well, Betty."

"Boy, you're too dramatic." FP shook his head, rueful. "Betty, tell him he's overreacting."

"Jug, you might be overreacting," I hedged. "I'll reserve judgment for now. Far be it from me to interfere in family matters, anyway. So how did this all even happen?" I was dying of curiosity, and from the looks on Pop's and Veronica's faces, I wasn't the only one.

"I still don't totally get it. You'll have to go directly to the source for the full story," Jughead said, nodding toward his dad.

FP swiveled on his stool so he could talk more directly to all of us at once. "I know Jug likes to think of himself as a loner, but that's not really true anymore, the way it once was."

It was a fair point. Jughead had a girlfriend, a regular group of friends (no matter how small and inner circle the four of us were). He was the leader of the Serpents—the polar opposite of an island unto himself. Sure, he liked to hang on the periphery of most mainstream types of experiences, but FP was right…somewhere over these past few years, Jughead Jones had evolved into less of a recluse and more of a cult figure.

"And, while no one's more surprised by this than yours truly, I am the sheriff of this town, and he's the sheriff's son. He's a symbol of this town, of leadership," FP said.

Jughead flashed a quick smirk. "Get this: I'm a symbol of the sunny promise of Riverdale's youth." He grinned again so that a dimple appeared on one cheek, actually looking the part of "sunny" for a fraction of a second, even though he was being totally ironic.

"Jughead Jones, brimming with sunshine and promise? Our very own J. D. Salinger? Interesting choice," Veronica quipped, taking a momentary look up from the diner's books. She wasn't kidding, but there was still plenty of affection behind her words.

"Trust me—I agree," Jughead replied. "What can I tell you? If you've got an issue with the decision, you're gonna have to take it up with the mayor. I think you know how to find her."

"What?" Veronica's dark eyebrows flew up. "This was my mom's idea?"

"One hundred percent. She's the one who talked to my dad."

"I tried to convince her Jughead wouldn't be up for it, but she wasn't taking no for an answer. Apparently, Lodge women are incredibly stubborn," FP said, raising his eyebrow.

"Yes, well…I can hardly argue that point," Veronica conceded.

"You weren't exaggerating, Jug," I said. "This is amazing. Beyond." I poked him in the rib and watched him smile and shrink back. "Honestly? I kind of can't wait to see you up there onstage."

"Alas," he said, "that's not going to happen."

"But—you said Mayor Lodge wouldn't take no for an answer…"

"Right, no. She wouldn't. I'm doing it; there's no way out. Trust me—I tried. What I meant was, you won't be watching me onstage. Because"—he added slyly, throwing a quick glance his father's way—"you'll be up there next to me the whole time."

"What?"

"You're his only hope, Betty. Hear the boy out," FP pleaded.

"Betts. You know me. Bad enough I got roped into this in the first place. There's no way I'm going up there alone. So I pointed out that with WRIV sponsoring the Revels and covering it, it only made sense to have their number one anchor's daughter up onstage with me."

Sneaky. "And I'm not at all shocked that my mom went along with it," I said. "Now that you bring it up, it's kind of funny that she didn't suggest it herself." My own mom wasn't one to miss an opportunity that landed in her lap. To put it kindly. Even if it was sort of an opportunity for me.

FP laughed. "Yeah, that's exactly what I said. But I guess she's been real caught up with that Farm of hers lately."

My stomach clenched at the mention. My mother being busy with the Farm was, sadly, unsurprising. My mother too busy to enjoy a moment in the spotlight? More of a curveball.

More proof of how insidious the Farm's grip on her was turning out to be.

"Pop, talk about a hashtag TBT," Veronica said suddenly, breaking through the momentary silence. "<u>What</u> is this institutional treasure and where have you been hiding it all this time?" She waved what appeared to be a large black-and-white photo, her eyes shining with glee.

"That?" Pop suddenly seemed almost bashful. "Just a picture of my great-grandfather with Riverdale's founding mayor. Where did you find it, anyway?" He reached to take it back, but Veronica shrunk away and passed it around.

"It was hiding underneath the ledger, and it's a <u>delightful</u> blast from the past. I don't know why this wouldn't be on display for all to see."

"You kids always have plenty of other stuff going on. Who cares about ancient history?"

I took a peek at the photo—there he was, Pop's great-grandfather, looking every bit like a carbon copy of Pop himself but for the period clothes. Same uniform, with its iconic apron and paper hat, same wide-cheeked smile, same warm eyes.

"But aren't the Revels all about history?" I said.

"That's exactly what they're all about," FP put in. "That's the whole point. And despite what Pop is implying, some people in this town are real eager to repeat history."

Was it my imagination, or did Pop's eyes darken for a fraction of a minute? It was a split-second moment, and then it was gone, before I could even decide if I'd seen what I thought I'd seen.

"Yes, well, be that as it may," Pop said, gathering the photo back after it had finished making the rounds and tucking it away under the counter again, "don't you all have a Revel to prepare for?"

Even me—no thanks to my mom, I thought. Hadn't Evelyn been leading the charge on all things Revels? Meaning that being part of the Farm didn't necessarily mean abstaining from town activities. "I guess we do," I said, the wheels still turning in my restless brain.

"Miles to go! And time capsules to open!" Jughead said. "So, what do you say, Betty? Up for standing beside me, representing the hope and future of Riverdale? I mean, between the two of us, you are the sunny one. Not to mention, my Serpent Queen." Jughead snapped me out of my reverie.

"I suppose that's true," I agreed. About being his queen, in any case, even if Dark Betty had cast a slight pall on my reputation for sunniness. "Juggie, you know I can't say no to you. Anyway, it's a time capsule. Opening it will be fun!"

I was trying to psych myself up. And if my own involvement somehow piqued my mother's curiosity and moved her even an inch farther away from that cult that had abducted her soul? Well, that would just be a bonus.

"It's so cute that you think that." Jughead took my hands in his. "Betty, this is <u>Riverdale</u>. There is no way that opening up a time capsule means opening anything other than a can of worms. And that's <u>best-case</u> scenario."

"I second that theory," Veronica said. "But hey—no matter what's in there, we can bet it won't be boring."

"No," I agreed. "Nothing around here ever is."

∧∧∧

Sweet Pea:

Hey! Psyched for Revels? You won't believe what I just heard.

Josie:

?

Sweet Pea:

It's Jug. The mayor got him roped into being the one to open the time capsule.

Josie:

Random. Seems like the least likely candidate.

Sweet Pea:

Totally. You'll be there, right? Singing?

Josie:

Doubt Moms would let me skip it. But I'm not singing until Thurs. Thank god.

Sweet Pea:

Why thank god? You love performing??

Josie:

Sure. But Mom wants me to bring the Pussycats out . . .

Sweet Pea:

And they're still freezing you out?

Josie:

Total cold war.

Sweet Pea:

What are u gonna do?

Josie:

What can I do? I mean, I guess I'll ask them. Who cares about my pride, right? Worst they can do is say no. Which is what I fully expect to happen. Just for the record.

Josie:

Nope. Actually, worse they can do is ghost me completely. Also not out of the question.

Sweet Pea:

Sorry. That's rough. You know I'm around if you want to vent.

Josie:

You're sweet. But I'm super busy preparing. And anyway, that's not what this is. You know that.

Sweet Pea:

It could be . . .

Josie:

Okay, just calm down, Romeo. ☺ I couldn't right now, even if I wanted to. Wish me luck. I gotta go try to wrangle some cats.

Sweet Pea:

👄 Ttyl

Josie:

👋 L8r.

∧∧∧

Josie:

Hey, divas . . . 👋

Josie:

How's it going?

Val:

What's going on, J?

Josie:

You guys busy?

Melody:

You know. Homework. Practice. The usual. Why?

Josie:

You've been playing?

63

Val:

I know you didn't think you were the only cat who could book a gig. You may be the in-house entertainment at that crazy faux New York "speakeasy," but you're not the only one of us who has talent.

Val:

Maybe you've forgotten already, but there's that sick venue outside Greendale that you always said wasn't worth our time. We decided you were wrong.

Melody:

BTW, they're cool. AND they pay better than any gig we had when the Pussycats were still together.

Josie:

Come on. OBVIOUSLY I know you guys are hella talented. And I'm sorry if you thought I got too bigheaded or whatever . . .

Melody:

Um, yeah. Whatever.

Val:

So what is it you wanted, Josie?

Josie:

Never mind. Have a good practice.

Melody:

Yeah. Take care.

Val:

Later, J.

Josie:

Sure.

CHAPTER FIVE

Archie:

Jug, Ronnie just told me. YOU'RE the MVP at the time capsule opening ceremony?

Jughead:

I know, it's so alarmingly mainstream.

Archie:

Well, I'll be cheering from the crowd. But I think my dad will actually be up there onstage with you. Andrews Construction is gonna be the one to wheel the time capsule out onto the pagoda.

Jughead:

It's good to know that if I have to die a banal, basic metaphorical death into average-Joe behavior, I'll be surrounded by my loved ones . . .

KEVIN

I was sitting on my bed, poring over the reading for English lit, when the door to my bedroom opened with a slow creak.

"Yes?" I looked up. Josie's dark curls appeared in the doorway.

"What's up, Josie?" I asked, putting down my book and sitting up straighter. "You look like how this homework is making me feel. I'm *definitely* not passing that quiz on Friday. Wait." A thought occurred to me. "Do you think the quiz will be canceled, now that the Revels is happening?"

She looked confused.

"Never mind. There's not a single teacher in school who would randomly let us off the hook just because of something like the Revels. That's dumb."

Was I still talking? *Reel it in, Kevin.* "It's also *definitely* not why you came in here. Forget it. So, what's going on?"

She sighed and settled herself at my desk, turning the chair so she was facing me. "Pussycat drama. Or, ex-Pussycat drama, to be more accurate. The girls are *still* not over my solo trip from last year. They are having absolutely none of me."

"Oh," I said, getting it. "You reached out and they shot you down?"

She gave a short, bitter laugh. "Uh, not *quite*. Shooting me down might have required some actual kindness or empathy.

These ladies were out for blood. It was more like . . . well, like cats toying with a trapped mouse." She shrugged. "I guess that's appropriate."

"I'm sorry," I said. "That stinks." It was an understatement; I knew how upset Josie was about the way things were with the Pussycats these days.

Our parents were only newly together, but since they'd gotten involved (involved again? Since I guess they'd been a "thing" in high school, which I *so* did not want to think about), Josie and I had been expected to quickly acclimate to life as a blended family. Was it awkward? Sure, at times. I don't think either of us ever expected to have nightly slumber parties for basically the rest of our high school days. But there were worse Marcia Bradys I could imagine playing foil to my Greg. Overall, we got along—we both wanted to see our parents happy, at the end of the day.

And we cared about each other, even if we didn't know each other that well yet. Now we were privy to each other's lives in a way we hadn't been—couldn't have been, of course—before. Which meant that I knew all about her rift with the Pussycats. And I knew that as much as Josie tried to put on a strong, fierce front, she missed her girls. *A lot.*

Was she wrong to try to strike out on her own? Honestly, probably not. Everyone who's ever heard her sing or watched her perform knows Josie is destined for something way bigger than life in Riverdale. Juilliard, maybe—she was auditioning for them this year—but I knew (we all did, really): even *that* would only be the beginning for Ms. Josephine McCoy.

She needed to evolve as an artist, to find her own two feet. But her friends weren't wrong to feel the way they did, either—they were hurt, being left behind in the dust. They had futures, too. And they'd thought they had a friend who was also a loyal bandmate.

It was a lousy situation. I could see everyone's side. But I understood why everyone was feeling so raw, too.

And I personally had a front-row seat to Josie's inner pain.

"Why were you even contacting them? No offense," I said. "But, I mean—you know they're still upset. Don't be a glutton for punishment. You know it won't end well."

She sighed. "Yeah. I know. *Trust me*, I know. But my mom . . ." She trailed off.

"Ah." It all made sense now. "Let me guess. She went all Ex-Mayor Momzilla, Esq. on you?" Sierra only wanted what was best for Josie, anyone with eyes could see that, but she was also . . . beyond intense.

Josie's eyes flashed. "She was the one who pushed me to go solo in the first place! She thought being in the 'Cats was holding me back, keeping me from 'shining as brightly as I could.' Those were actually her words!" Josie gestured while she talked, getting more frantic as she got more upset.

"And she has a point, even if it's a small one—we all know my dream has always been to make it as a performer. So I did what she suggested. Even though it was hard as *hell*. Because when it comes to my career, I did *not* come to play."

"Nor should you." Sometimes being around Josie was like being around the living embodiment of an inspirational meme in the best possible way. I just wanted to stand up and sing some Beyoncé or Katy Perry anthems with her.

But I was getting distracted again. Now wasn't the time.

Her hands moved faster as her voice rose. "And great, maybe my songwriting is developing. Maybe my sound is going in some new directions, with no outside influences to interfere with my flow. Sure. That's all good. But—truth?"

"Always," I said, even though I knew where she was going with this.

"I miss my friends." She blinked, her eyes growing watery for a minute.

I took her hand. "Of course you do. And if it makes you feel any better, I'm sure they miss you, too. They wouldn't be so angry if they didn't, right? The opposite of love isn't hate; it's indifference. I think I read that on a yogurt smoothie bottle cap once."

She pulled back, straightening her spine and trying to get her composure back. "Maybe," she sniffed. "I don't know. But *Mom* was the one who told me to ditch them, and then Mom was the one who *insisted* I convince them to perform with me. At the Revels."

"Oh, *yikes*," I said, feeling outraged on her behalf. "So much nope. Unacceptable. Doesn't she know you have your pride?"

"Apparently not," Josie said. "And anyway, I *don't* have my pride. Not anymore. Mom wouldn't let it go. You know how she can be."

I nodded. "Who among us hasn't been on the wrong side of a patented Sierra McCoy steely gaze?" And I *lived* with her now. So I knew firsthand.

"What else could I do? I texted the girls."

"And they weren't into it?"

"They were *so* not into it, they were practically living in a different zip code." Her eyes welled up again. "They were all about how they've been picking up gigs in Greendale, without me, since we split."

"Ouch," I said, choosing not to remind her that she'd been taking gigs on her own, too. Which had kind of been the whole plan, all along.

Josie shifted in the chair, resigned. She wasn't one for slumped shoulders, but that was the vibe she was giving off. "Needless to say," she went on, "the Pussycats *won't* be scheduling their reunion tour for the Riverdale Revels. Mom is just going to have to deal."

"She will." *What choice did she have?* "And besides—a Josie McCoy solo show is nobody's consolation prize." I smiled at her. "It's going to be awesome."

She gave a tiny grin to match mine. "Thanks, Kev. But the thing is, I was kind of hoping it *wouldn't* be a solo show."

"I'm sure Cheryl would perform with you," I said. "When has that girl *ever* turned down a moment in the spotlight?"

Josie laughed. "Yeah, I'm sure she would. But I was actually sort of thinking . . . *you'd* do it?"

"What?" I was surprised, and then I overplayed that surprise just to tease her. I shot her a serious, questioning look. "Josie McCoy, are you proposing a duet?"

"Kevin Keller, that's exactly what I'm proposing." For a moment, she hesitated. "If you're up for it. I mean, I've heard you sing in the school musicals; I *know* you've got the goods."

"If you're expecting me to feign a false modesty, that's not going to happen," I assured her. "I have too much respect for the both of us. It would be a waste of our valuable time."

"Agreed," she said, smiling full-on now.

I hated to burst her bubble. "Unfortunately, even though I would *so* love to do it, I won't be able to."

Josie's face fell, and I hurried to clarify. "If you'd asked sooner, maybe—but the thing is, my dad is actually *in* the motorcade. He'll be driving his original sheriff car, Mayor Lodge insisted, and I know he's actually, really kind of weirdly excited about it."

"And you told him you'd ride with him." She nodded, understanding.

"Yep. I mean . . ." I felt my mouth twist with guilt. "He's my *dad*. And he was *so* into it. And I wouldn't be able to do both. We need to be behind the wheel before the music starts, and there's all sorts of behind-the-scenes things happening beforehand, too."

She stood up, her face stony with resolve. "I totally get it, Kevin. And I appreciate you saying that you would have been up for it."

"It's the truth." I stood up, too. Impulsively, I gave her a hug.

"I gotta say, Kev," she started, "I was not looking for a step-brother at this point in my life. But . . . you make a good one."

"Thanks, Josie," I said. "You, too. We're in this together."

"Good luck with the English," she said, moving to the door. "I definitely think we're still having that quiz."

"Yeah," I said. "I know."

As far as almost-stepsisters went, I had a pretty smart one. It sucked that she was feeling so alone right now. I definitely knew that feeling.

I know I'm lucky. My parents love me—even if they can't love me together, like as a couple—I have good friends, and when no one is actively trying to stalk and murder my friends or me, life in Riverdale is pretty good. Even my blended family is more *Brady Bunch* than *Dynasty*. I'm mostly happy.

But sometimes, I'm still . . . lonely. Even with all of that, with all of *them*.

Betty had Jughead. Veronica had Archie. Even Cheryl Blossom, reigning terror of Riverdale High, had found her love connection.

When would it be my turn?

Joaquin is out of the picture . . . and so is Moose, at least until he's in a place where he feels comfortable being out, period, never mind being out with me. I'm trying to give him space, because I get it, it's a personal choice, and it's not my place to rush him. But that hurts, too.

I mean, is it me?

Once upon a time, I wouldn't have let myself go there. But it's getting harder to stay positive.

I know Veronica thinks the pageant is ridiculous (she hasn't made much of a secret of that). I know she's helping only because I completely begged her to. But I'll take it. The pageant sounds fun, and I'm lonely. I'll take any help I can get.

These days, I feel like I really need a win.

∿∿∿

It wasn't like my friends didn't care. They understood how hard it was for me—dating, meeting eligible bachelors in a one-maple-tap town like Riverdale. I suspected the mailman was gay, but he was, like, five thousand years old and wore dad sneakers unironically. My options were pretty limited.

Internet dating was stressful. Veronica wanted to set up a profile for me, but I balked when she suggested using a shot of Archie's abs in place of my own. "Sick burn, Ronnie," I told her.

"Creative editing," she said. "It's the American way." But I refused, and so plan B it was.

"We're going to that gay club," Betty told me. "Innuendo? On the edge of town?"

"We can't get in. It's over twenty-one," I protested.

Veronica waved a hand. "Please." She turned on her heel and started strutting down the hallway, leaving me and Betty scrambling to keep up in her wake.

We stopped when we found Reggie at his locker. He was totally amused by Veronica's request. "What do you three squares want with fake IDs?"

Veronica tossed her hair over her shoulder. "Putting aside the fact that you seem to be overlooking my entirely well-earned reputation as an urban sophisticate—with all the requisite recreational debauchery that entails—"

"Yeah, yeah," Reggie said mildly.

"—I'm going to need you to step outside your privileged heteronormative bubble for a millisecond." She put her hands on her hips. "Do you even know how hard it is for Kevin to meet guys here in Riverdale?"

"We *need* to get him into a gay bar," Betty put in. It made me sound not unlike a pathetic charity case, but whatever—it seemed to be working.

Reggie stroked his chin, doing his best impression of "pensive." "Not being able to get action, like, *ever*?" he mused. "That must suck, bro."

"Pretty much," I said. *Like I needed reminding?*

He put a hand on my shoulder in what I assume was meant to be reassuring. "I'll make you an ID, Keller. Foolproof. On the house."

Relief flooded me. "Thank you, Reggie. Truly. I will totally get you back."

He chuckled. "Dude—I don't need any help from you."

"Of course not."

"Oh, Reggie," Veronica sang, "while you're at it—will you pretty please make one for Betty and me?"

Turns out, Reggie Mantle can never say no to Veronica Lodge. Lucky for us.

∿∿∿

We made a plan, and I made a mental note to thank the powers that be again for delivering me such amazing friends. When I asked Betty and Veronica if they were sure—like, what would they even do at a gay bar while I was supposedly on the prowl?—Veronica had the perfect response right at her perfectly manicured fingertips.

"Are you kidding me? One: dance without getting drooled on by gross straight guys. Two: relive the best of the holy quartet."

"The holy quartet?" Betty asked.

Veronica ticked them off on her fingers. "Gaga. Britney. Cher. And Madonna."

"Royalty if not necessarily religion," I agreed.

"I'm not finished," Veronica said. "Three: glitter everywhere."

"I do love glitter," Betty said.

"Who doesn't?" Veronica and I said, in unison.

It was settled. And there was a small part of me—very small, but still there, still real—that was kind of excited.

∧∧∧

Scratch that. "I'm filled with dread," I said.

Innuendo loomed before us, its marquis glaring and bright, seemingly bigger than the Hollywood sign, though I knew that wasn't possible. A line of what was mostly guys snaked down the sidewalk, everyone doing their best to appear nonchalant, bored even, and not like they were secretly fearing being turned away at the door.

Or maybe they were nonchalant. Maybe I was the only one with this constant, gnawing insecurity turning backflips in my stomach like a contortionist.

I didn't think so, though.

Of course, if there was one person who was totally impervious to insecurity and doubt, it was Veronica. She strode with purpose toward the front of the line, arms swinging along with the hem of her purple Versace minidress. Her shoes flashed a peek of that signature red sole with every click of her daggerlike stiletto heels.

From beside her, Betty stuffed her hands into her pockets. "I feel underdressed," she said, though she didn't really sound worried. She'd taken down her iconic ponytail for the occasion, but she wore dark skinny jeans and a lacy black top, which was about as "edgy" as Betty got—when she wasn't cosplaying her darker self, that is. Not that it mattered—it worked for her.

As for me, I'd let Veronica dress me in a slimmer sweater and jeans than I'd normally wear. When I protested that I felt like a "metrosexual fraud," she insisted that I was pulling it off. And there was a small part of me (okay, not that small) that wanted to believe her.

Instinctively, I started to hunch up the closer we got to the bouncer. But Ronnie was incredible—she only stood up straighter, throwing her shoulders back with the determination of someone who's never known a moment of doubt or rejection. I knew it wasn't true—there was that whole scandal with her father back in the city, after all, where she was basically a social pariah, however briefly. But lesson learned: Fake it till you make it. I tried to walk with the same confident gait.

"Good evening," Veronica said, smiling at the bouncer. He eyed us in a manner that was not *not* welcoming. But Veronica

forged ahead, undaunted. She leaned in and whispered something to him. I strained to hear—Betty did, too—but to no
avail.

After a beat, the bouncer stepped back. I sighed, preparing to
retreat with as much dignity as I could muster. Instead, something
miraculous happened.

He unclipped the velvet rope and ushered us through. "Enjoy
your night."

Veronica led the way, tossing the bouncer a little wave over her
shoulder as she did.

I grabbed Betty by the elbow as we followed. "How'd she *do*
that?"

"We'll never know," she said simply.

We went inside.

⌃⌃⌃

Veronica wasn't wrong. There was Gaga. There was Madonna.
There was even some Kesha and Kylie Minogue that slipped onto
the playlist, for a hot minute or two. We sang along at the top of our
lungs, totally free and uncaring about being or looking cool or,
frankly, being anyone other than who we were in that exact moment,
at that exact time and place. The space was crowded, dark and
humid and alive with the smell of total abandon—or at least, that's
how it felt to me.

Okay, fine, I was finally at a gay bar and, somehow, I was still attached at the hip to my friends, but it was thrilling, enervating nonetheless.

Until it wasn't.

I had made it, into Innuendo, dressed to kill (as Veronica assured me), fake ID in hand, belting Cher at the top of my lungs. If there was a checklist for my first truly authentic gay outing, I'd ticked all the boxes. It was fun, sure, but it was also hot. And sweaty. And starting to feel a little claustrophobic.

Maybe it was *too much* fun for me? Maybe I'm just not . . . wired for it?

The thought was depressing—was I, like, *destined* to be lonely and single until my end of days?—and I slipped away, to the bar.

"Can I get a ginger ale?" I didn't care what my ID said; I didn't need to add drinking to this mix. It was already starting to feel like a slow-release train wreck. Alcohol wouldn't make that better.

I was sipping my (totally G-rated) drink, watching a shiny red cherry bob up and down in the fizzy liquid, when I felt a hand on my shoulder.

"What are you doing here, by yourself? We didn't even see you slip away." It was Betty. Veronica was on her heels, her forehead glistening. She fanned herself dramatically with one hand.

"Trying to hydrate," I said, taking a deliberate sip.

"Hydrate later!" Veronica instructed. "There are at least fifty hot guys here just waiting to be flirted with."

"Not with me they're not," I said, finally admitting it to myself and to my friends. Even in a gay bar, my fabulous gal pals attracted ten times more attention on the dance floor than I did. Maybe it *was* me.

I took another sip of my drink but then pushed it away, the cloying sweetness sticking at the back of my throat. "Sorry, girls. We tried. And I appreciate it. But . . . this isn't my scene."

"Maybe we didn't try hard enough," Veronica countered.

"Come back for one more dance, at the very least!" Betty said, earnest and eager.

I didn't want to be a bummer. But I had to be honest. "I'm sorry," I said. "I don't want to grind up on strangers. It's not me. I don't know what I expected would happen here. But this wasn't it."

I sighed. Even though I was finally—finally!—surrounded by other gay people (aka the thing I wanted literally more than *anything*), I'd never felt more alone.

"Okay," Betty said, slowly seeing that I wasn't just exaggerating or being melodramatic. "So what next?"

"No, you two stay," I insisted. "Have fun. You're having a good time. I don't need to ruin your night. I'm going to go home and watch *The Matchelorette*. I hear Kelsey gets kicked out of the champagne sauna tonight."

"Spoiler alert!" Veronica protested. "But okay. If you're sure."

"*So* sure."

"Brunch tomorrow at Pop's?" Betty suggested.

"Definitely."

∿∿∿

I thought about stopping by Fox Forest on my way home—old habits die hard, and for a long time after I first came out, it was the only place I felt like I could be my true self. When I felt alone, it was a place to meet other people like me. Sometimes we just talked. Sometimes, more. I'd met a few closeted guys—I'm not naming names—but we all knew everything changed when Jason Blossom was murdered. I may be lonely, but I definitely don't have a death wish.

So, instead, I went home. Dad was up when I got in, settled on the couch with a bowl of popcorn and the remote in hand. He looked surprised to see me. "Thought you were sleeping at Betty's."

"I bailed," I said, closing the door behind me. "We all snuck into a gay bar."

If Dad was scandalized, he didn't show it at all. "Doesn't look like you had a very good time," he observed.

"I didn't," I admitted. "I left early."

Dad gave me a look and gestured to the space beside him on the couch. I sat down, resting my hands on my knees. "The bar was filled with guys, Dad," I started.

"And you didn't meet someone nice, your age?" he guessed.

"No. And I have this sinking feeling that I never will." The thought was too unbearable. My throat tightened at the words.

Dad took a deep breath, obviously thinking hard about how to navigate this Important Parenting Moment. Credit where credit is due—he always tries.

"Listen, Kevin," he began. "I can't tell you *when* it'll happen for you—college, when you move to New York for your Broadway career—"

"My what now?"

"—who the heck knows?"

"Very inspiring," I joked.

"But one thing I *do* know? You're not gonna be alone, kiddo." He grabbed me in a manly sort of one-armed hug.

Cheesy as it sounds, even though it solved exactly none of my problems, that hug from my dad   coupled with a hefty dose of empathy—meant everything. And it made me feel worlds better. No matter how alone I felt in my dating life, I wasn't alone in life-life. Friends and family weren't romance, but they weren't nothing. Not by any stretch.

I swiped the remote from his side. "*Barefoot Contessa?* Or *Great British Bake Off?*"

"I was watching that mystery series, Kevin," he said, before relenting. "What about that *Matchelorette?* With the sauna where they all drink too much?"

I flipped the channel and helped myself to some of his popcorn. It was still warm.

"Did glitter just fall out of your hair?" he asked, bewildered.

"Probably."

He laughed. After a minute, I did, too.

∧∧∧

My door clicked in its doorjamb as Josie left. I heard her retreat to her bedroom, and after a minute, I heard the smooth sound of her vocal exercises, her deep, sweet voice skipping up and down the scales. It was soothing, and a nice reminder: No matter how I felt, no matter how brutal the dating world had been—I *wasn't* alone.

Innuendo had been a bust. Online dating was traumatizing. And I'd vowed to myself and my loved ones that I'd never go cruising in Fox Forest again. So maybe that all added up to a little more time being single.

But Dad was right—who cares, anyway? It's not *that* big of a deal.

I had friends and family who love me; I was just getting started.

CHAPTER SIX

Veronica:

Hey, Archiekins: Can I ask impose on you for a huge favor?

Archie:

Any time. You know that.

Veronica:

It turns out I'm a little shorthanded for accepting delivery of the drinks for tonight's after-party. Reggie is apparently "training" in preparation for the pageant, lifting with Chuck Clayton and some of the other Bulldogs who are signed up. He wants to be—and I quote—"ripped AF."

Archie:

He knows there actually ISN'T a swimsuit portion, right?

Veronica:

And yet.

Veronica:

Anyway, I have some Serpents around to help, and I hate to be the cliche of a damsel in distress, but I could really use your broad shoulders for a half hour or two.

Archie:

You can have as much of me for as long as you want. Just have to finish helping Dad dig up the time capsule for tonight. It's so old—it's a delicate job.

Veronica:

I thought your dad had done that already.

Archie:

He tried to. But apparently he had to get the map to its exact location from Pop, and he wasn't around until this afternoon.

Veronica:

Pop? That seems random.

Archie:

Yeah, I guess. Hey—Dad's calling. See you soon?

Of course! 💋

XOXO

∧∧∧

JUGHEAD

At 5:45 p.m., the Pickens Park pagoda was buzzing with the low-key—but no less sincere—hum of curiosity that kicks into gear whenever anything out of the usual takes place in a town as allegedly sleepy as Riverdale.

If there had been any doubt about how people would react to the Revels, it was gone now. The Revels were not only a celebration of Riverdale itself, but they were something new, something different, and (presumably) murder-free.

Streamers festooned the autumnal foliage of the maple trees, and brassy big-band music wafted from a huge speaker adjacent to the pagoda. Everyone had come out for the big time capsule opening, and from the look on Mayor Lodge's face, she was thrilled with the turnout.

As for me, I was curious, I guess—I couldn't totally deny it, much as I wanted to maintain my nonchalant distance—but I can't say I was quite at the "buzzing" stage. Generally speaking, buzzing isn't really my style. And neither was being up here, front and center, on the pagoda itself, staring out at a gaggle of eager Revelers.

I looked out to see a mosaic of faces peering back at me, eager: Pop Tate, mild and vaguely inscrutable. Principal Weatherbee, with his typical reserve. Evelyn Evernever, intense as ever. In one cluster, my Serpents, leather jackets bobbing, trying to seem above it all but clearly a little bit curious themselves.

Betty stood beside me, grinning away hard enough (and with enough genuine joy, god bless her) to make up for my general lack of pep. To my left was Dad, decked out for the occasion in his sheriff's uniform—the proximate cause of my involvement in all this, in the first place. Alice Cooper had her crew positioned precisely to the right of the stage, boom mics and floodlights swinging just out of frame, beams of illumination bright enough to make me squint. And at the podium, presiding calmly over it all, was Mayor Hermione Lodge.

"Feeling spirited and youthful?" Betty asked, sotto voce.

"Have those words *ever* been used to describe me?" I challenged.

Archie, who'd been front and center, grinning away at me, stepped forward. "You got this, man."

"*Does* he, though?" Cheryl Blossom's cut-glass voice broke through the murmurs of the crowd. "We're already at least seven minutes behind schedule. As a member of one of this town's founding families, I'm eager to see what's inside this little relic of yesteryear. And *then* I want to make haste to La Bonne Nuit to enjoy some quality conviviality with my paramour."

"Cher, *chill,*" Toni muttered, not looking at all perturbed. After all, she was more than used to Cheryl by now. "It's not Jughead's fault the schedule slipped by seven minutes."

"Always so willing to stay positive, Toni. No wonder you're my better half," Cheryl relented.

Toni gave her a quick kiss on the cheek, then turned her attention back to the pagoda as Mayor Lodge moved closer to her microphone.

"Welcome, all of you, citizens of Riverdale," she began, her voice low and smooth. "From the entire mayor's office and city council, we're thrilled to be reviving the Riverdale Revels, beginning with the opening of our Jubilee time capsule. As you know by now, the Revels are a uniquely Riverdale-esque tradition, a celebration that I personally hope our town will continue to embrace for decades to come, much as our ancestors enjoyed it for so many bygone decades. The Revels are meant to be a true embodiment of the very best of Riverdale, and of course, the best of Riverdale begins and ends with all of you.

"Riverdale has always been defined by its citizens, and historically, our population has been a source of great pride. Now"— her voice dipped, indicating a change in tone, a slightly darker take on our own bizarro Brigadoon—"of course, events of the last few years have certainly tested our strength and our virtue as a community."

Next to me, Betty stifled a laugh, which almost prompted me to laugh, too. I bit my cheek hard to keep the urge at bay. Mayor Lodge definitely had that "adults of Riverdale" gift of either understating or—more common—completely denying the obvious. All our parents did. It was downright eerie, almost like it was some unspoken agreement.

(That felt way too paranoid. Right?)

"But I know we can come back from recent tragedies stronger than ever, and the newly reinaugurated Revels are my way of showing how much I appreciate you, my constituents." She smiled benevolently, and it was easy to see why she and her husband were so adroit at the delicate art of persuasion. (Even if Hiram's methods were notoriously more, ahem . . . *aggressive*, on occasion.)

Across the park, people smiled and cheered. They were drinking her in, eating the whole performance up with a spoon.

"Now, with my newly appointed sheriff, FP Jones, beside me—before all of *you*—who better to represent Riverdale's commitment to the promise of a vibrant future than our youth itself? Specifically, here to open the time capsule left for *our* generation, generations of Revels ago, we have Forsythe Pendleton Jones the Third."

She raised her hands and offered a graceful little "golf clap" in my direction, prompting the rest of the folks in the crowd to follow suit. I could hear the cheers from Veronica, Archie, and even Mr. Andrews behind me. I felt a furious blush creeping up the back of my neck; I couldn't remember the last time anyone had called me by my full given name. (And, really—is it any wonder?)

Hermione gestured that I should step to the microphone, and beside me, Betty gave my hand a squeeze. I took the opportunity to drag her forward with me, which finally did cause that bubbling giggle to erupt. The crowd laughed, too. The sense of relief, of joy and lightness—it was palpable, a feeling like we could all maybe, finally, breathe a sigh of relief, even—could it be?—*smile*, after so many murders, so much violence, so much darkness.

"Joining him is Elizabeth Cooper, who you all know from, among other things, her heartfelt toast at our 75th Anniversary Jubilee. Her mother, of course, is Alice Cooper, a dedicated neighbor whose commitment to providing truth and insight to our town—first, through the *Riverdale Register*, and now, via her whip-smart reportage on WRIV—has never wavered."

Hermione waved at Alice, who waved back in a gesture that was as close to humble as Alice got. Betty smiled tightly at her mom, and she and I took our places at the podium as Fred Andrews and his crew eased the time capsule out of the hole beneath an enormous maple tree where it had been laid to rest all those years ago.

It was a huge, weathered barrel of what had once been Blossom Maple Farms syrup; the logo was just visible beneath decades of dirt encrusted to the sides. As Mr. Andrews wheeled the time capsule toward us on the stage, a charge of energy filled the air: curiosity, maybe, or even eagerness, which was a new feeling for so many of us. The excavation had begun earlier today, not long after the school assembly, with Fred Andrews and his crew working in conscientious shifts, so that the progress was highly visible and closely monitored by us all.

(Even those of us who were feigning less interest in the whole thing.)

To be fair—it was impossible not to have at least a morbid curiosity, what with a relic of our past being literally unearthed before our very eyes.

I'd meant what I'd said to Betty—there was no way we weren't leaping straight into Pandora's box—but I, for one, was dying to see what was inside.

"We're so glad to be here," Betty said, taking over the microphone. She knows that, for the most part, I'm only a wordsmith from behind the comfort of a keyboard. "Thank you so much for giving us the honor of kicking off the Revels with the opening of the time capsule!"

She glanced at me, prompting me to add at least the bare minimum to her tiny speech. I leaned in. "Thanks," I agreed. "Also, you can just call me 'Jughead.'" Another collective chuckle floated through the air.

Mr. Andrews propped the barrel upright right in front of us and took a crowbar from a crew member who was waiting just beyond the stage.

"Are you ready?" he asked.

Betty and I nodded, and the crowd cheered again. Cheryl's eyes lit up as she took in the Blossom seal stamped onto the side of the barrel, still prominent enough to be recognizable after all these years.

He forced the crowbar under the lip of the barrel and grunted, leaning his weight into the movement. The wood at the barrel's seal crumbled.

For a minute, Mr. Andrews's face tightened, cords on his neck standing out like road map markings. I had a split second to worry that the cover to the barrel wouldn't come off, that our first official Revels event would belly flop spectacularly, and that somehow, it would feel like mine and Betty's fault, even though it so clearly wouldn't be; there were so many others here, with us, part of this, even now.

Then Mr. Andrews gave another loud groan of effort and heaved himself, really putting his shoulder into it. The barrel gave a little sigh of its own, something like a cranky cat, and then the cover slid off.

Betty's playful grip on my hand went tight enough that my knuckles cracked, and her eyes flew open, wider than I'd ever seen them.

"What's—"

I heard a collective gasp from the crowd as I followed her gaze. The cover had slid from the barrel, yes, but at the same time, the barrel itself tilted, sending Mr. Andrews back so he lost his grip. The entire thing rolled to one side and landed, heavy, with the soggy thud of rotted-out lumber, crumbling across the stage as the earth it contained spilled in every direction.

"Oh my god," Betty whispered.

That was when the screaming started.

It was Hermione, I realized—but only later, only in hindsight, when replaying the whole macabre scene back to myself, trying to puzzle some sense out of it all. Of course, it made perfect sense, though. Once the proverbial dust cleared and we'd all had a good, hard glimpse at the mess on the ground. And realized what had rattled Betty so badly. Realized exactly what we were all seeing.

It was a body.

Long-dead—little more than bones and worms by now, which shifted and squirmed in the dirt, respectively, announcing some hideous window into yet another sliver of Riverdale's past that would have been better left alone, buried.

Long-dead, sure. But no less ominous.

It was a pile of bones, jumbled, yellowing, and the tattered remains of—a dress? a ribbon?—something once floral, printed, now faded and streaked with grime, moldy and moth-eaten.

At the top of the heap, a skull winked out at us, a few strands of scraggly hair trailing in the dirt.

I stared, riveted, my gaze flickering from the bones, to Betty, slowly but surely steeling herself again.

"What the hell is it, Jug?" she whispered, her voice choked and raspy.

She didn't want an answer of course: She already had one. So I didn't say anything. Just wrapped an arm around her and concentrated on staying upright myself, reeling all the while.

PART TWO: REVENGE

CHAPTER SEVEN

FP Jones:

Your boy Curdle Junior's asking when I can come by to read his preliminary report of the body.

Hermione Lodge:

Not a body, FP. Bones. Remains. And that's assuming they are, actually, human remains.

FP Jones:

Curdle will have more information after his initial exam.

Hermione Lodge:

Nonetheless, it's early to jump to conclusions. And while I do appreciate your . . . enthusiasm for the job, Sheriff, you needn't worry. We've brought in some outside investigators to take over so that your attention can remain focused on the Revels. There's still so much planning to be done!

FP Jones:

You're very considerate, Madam Mayor.

Hermione Lodge:

Thank you.

FP Jones:

Thank YOU.

⌒⌒⌒

Hermione Lodge:

The natives are restless, Hiram. This Revels was supposed to be a boost for the town—not another dark secret.

Hiram Lodge:

Natives? I think you mean your constituents.

Hermione Lodge:

I mean our NEIGHBORS. And I can't say I blame them entirely. It was a gruesome scene.

Hiram Lodge:

Mi amor, I told you—don't worry. My men will take care of this. There are plenty of reasonable ways to play this one. Keep in mind—the original Revels dropped off the town calendar 75 years ago, and no one seems to know why. If there's one thing this town is good at, it's a cover-up.

I hope so. We can't afford a slip right now. The Revels need to go off without a single hitch.

Hiram Lodge:

Leave it to me.

∿∿∿

ARCHIE

I had to hand it to Veronica: When things went upside down, she really was her mother's daughter. And I meant that in the best possible way. No matter what came at her, Veronica always stood strong and powered through. The Revels' opening ceremony was no exception.

Immediately after the time capsule was opened, it was total pandemonium, I mean, we'd seen death in Riverdale—too much of it, recently—but I guess on some level, we'd been operating on the idea that evil was a newer side to life here in this town. Just a bunch of random, unfortunate, isolated instances. Were we kidding ourselves? Being deliberately delusional? Sure, maybe. But it was way more appealing than the alternative.

A body buried in a time capsule? That was different. That was old-school evil, literally planted in the ground for future generations to find.

Hermione snapped into action, though, with a quick but solemn announcement that of course the identity of the body would be investigated "thoroughly."

"But for now," she said, "we don't have the full story, and it would be wise not to panic and assume the worse. I think it best that we adjourn to La Bonne Nuit, as per our original plan, and allow ourselves some revelry despite this unexpected twist."

"'Unexpected twist,'" Veronica had scoffed to me. "God, my parents really do have the gift of spin." She sounded totally repulsed. "It was a *body in a barrel—a time capsule, no less*—but nope, nothing to see here."

I took her hand. "What now?"

"What now?" She squared her shoulders. "Archiekins, I've never been much of a thespian, but nonetheless, the old saying would serve us well at this moment: The show must go on."

I was stunned. I looked around—at the police tape perimeter FP was currently stringing up around us, at the little pile of dirt left on the pagoda from when the barrel had first tipped over . . . At the sight of my own dad's face, totally stricken by what he'd just seen. "Ronnie, you're seriously still having the after-party?"

"I don't have much choice, do I?" she said. "My mother just announced it to the crowd. But look." She gestured, indicating all the people who were currently wandering off, slowly and dazedly making their way to their cars. "After what just happened? These people *deserve* a party."

"I hear you, but—"

"But nothing." She waved me off. "You heard my mother. *It's too soon to panic.* This party is happening. We may as well get on the train, since it's way too late to get off the tracks. It'll be worse if we're not there."

"I . . . guess that's an okay reason?"

"It's a fine reason," she conceded. "But truthfully, it's not my only—or even my primary—objective. The thing is, Archie? My *mom* is going to the party. As we speak. So if I want to pin her down on how exactly she plans to sweep this little catastrophe under the rug, that's the place to do it. In a contained environment, where she can't easily dodge me. Before the cleaners have finished their dirty work."

So Veronica went into her own get-it-done mode, and there we were at La Bonne Nuit. Hermione did her best, making the rounds and shaking hands and nodding very seriously, but unsurprisingly, no one was feeling all that festive. The music felt too loud and the half-empty room was awkward. I kept thinking back to the horrified look on Betty's face when the barrel first tipped over. To the way she went unsteady on her feet. To the way my father staggered back from the barrel in total shock. I mean, I've seen my father *shot*, right in front of me—and I swear, I'd never seen an expression like the one on his face when the time capsule opened and that body came tumbling out.

Someone pushed a tumbler of amber liquid into my hand. "Bro, drink up. We could all use one tonight."

"Thanks, Reggie."

He wasn't bartending tonight; he'd only just grabbed a drink from the tray of a passing cocktail waitress.

"I'm okay, though." I passed it back to him. I wanted a clear head, especially for Ronnie.

She was in the far corner of the room with her mother, who she'd managed to pull aside. Both were trying to be as discreet as they could, but their body language was beyond tense.

"I'll take that." I looked up to see Fangs Fogarty reach for the drink eagerly. He raised it in a small *cheers* to Reggie before taking a sip. "That was pretty messed up, back there at the pagoda."

"Please. For this town? That was so banal it's almost quaint." Cheryl sidled up with Toni, the three of them making a wall of Serpent leather and worried looks. I noticed Cheryl's little throwaway sarcastic comment didn't match the tense crease between her eyebrows.

"The real *Twilight Zone* sitch on our hands?" She went on,

sipping daintily at something bubbly and pink. "The fact that this party is even still happening. So weird."

"*So* weird," Kevin said, entering our little circle.

"Definitely not of the normal," Toni agreed.

"Mayor Lodge wants people feeling reassured," I tried to explain, even though in my heart I didn't really buy it myself. "She thought this was the best way. It's like Veronica told me, 'The show must go on.'"

"Hmm." Cheryl eyed me. "Somehow, chum, there is a smack of conviction lacking in your words. And based on what I can see?" She glanced over to where Veronica and her mother were still talking, both of them looking way more upset now. Arms were waving and faces were looking very pinched. "Your *petite copine* has her doubts as well."

I didn't have much of an answer to that.

Saved by the bell, though. From just outside the ladies' room, Betty caught my eye and waved me toward her.

"Excuse me for a second," I said to the group.

"Fear not, Galahad, this fete will most assuredly be over before you can come back."

As I moved away, I heard Kevin respond, "We can only hope."

⌒⌒⌒

"Hey," I said, craning to Betty to talk over the weirdly loud music. "What's up?"

"Nothing," she said. "You just had a deer-in-headlights look on your face and I thought maybe you could use a smooth exit."

I smiled, grateful. "You thought right. Man, I want to have Veronica's back tonight—I mean, I *do* have her back, always— but they're not wrong about the vibe in here right now. I really don't think this is what anyone had in mind when they thought of an after-party."

Betty shrugged. "And I really don't think a jumble of bones was what *anyone* had in mind when they thought of opening a time capsule. And yet, here we are. Irony, thy name is Riverdale." Her lips curled into a hint of a smile. It was definitely the best she could do.

"But speaking of having V's back—and graceful exits—do we think *she* needs to be rescued from her mother?" Her eyes darted over to Veronica and her mom, not waving their arms quite as much, but still pretty worked up.

"The good news is, no one's really even paying attention," I said. "Everyone's pretty much caught up in their own thing right now. Look." I pointed. It was Penelope Blossom, stirring her own drink with a look of . . . well, I couldn't tell. Boredom? Distraction? She didn't *seem* all that stressed about the body. But then again, if there was anyone in this town who would take that kind of thing in stride, it was her.

"Betty, such a kind soul. Always wanting to rescue people."

We turned, and there was Evelyn, her curly brown hair bouncing at her shoulders and looking super intently at Betty. The words she was speaking were friendly, but the tone she was using, less so.

Betty gave a tight smile. "Hello, Evelyn. Fancy meeting you here."

"The mayor herself said the after-party was still on. Of course I'd come by. I'm so thrilled to share the Revels with the town of Riverdale."

"It is . . . thrilling," Betty said, obviously fighting back an eye roll.

"Betty." Evelyn reached out a hand to Betty's arm, and Betty flinched. "I just wish—and I know your mom and sister both wish, too—that you could be more open-minded."

Betty's eyes went dark. "Listen to me carefully, Evelyn. I know you think you've got all the dirt on my family. Because of my mom's and Polly's testimonies. But believe me when I tell you: *You. Know. Nothing.*"

Evelyn pulled back, blinking. "Hmm. I think you'll find that's not the case." She smiled again. "Either way—it's nice to see that your impulses are always to be helpful. I wonder what would happen if you directed those energies in a more positive, productive direction? I bet it would be glorious."

"Like the direction of the Farm, you mean?"

"I didn't say that. But that's a very good example. Why n—ouch!"

Abruptly, someone bumped Evelyn from behind, sending her bag off her shoulder and onto the ground. Girl things scattered everywhere—at least a half-dozen tubes of lipstick, jars of face cream, those compact powder/mirror things, and two different mini cans of hair spray. Evelyn didn't even look like the kind of girl who wore much makeup, but it just went to show, I didn't know everything, either.

Betty dropped down to help her pick it all up, sighing. She seemed way more concerned with seeing Evelyn on her way than with the weirdness of the contents of Evelyn's bag in the first place.

I mean: valid. And compared to the other things we've seen tonight, I guess it wasn't actually all that weird. Hair spray was pretty tame, in the grand scheme of things.

"See?" Evelyn said when they were finished and both standing up again. "So helpful, Betty. Although"—her voice went low—"I have to say, people in this town really should be more careful."

"See you later, guys!" she said, suddenly cheerful, leaving Betty and me standing together, unsettled.

"Be more careful?" I said as soon as she was gone. "That was weird. It almost sounded like . . . a threat."

"Yeah," Betty said, fists clenched. "It did."

∧∧∧

FINALLY ready to duck out of here—if I should still meet you at La Bonne Nuit?

Evelyn:

Actually, the after-party is not really happening. I'm pretty sure it's going to end any minute. So honestly, I don't think you need to bother. I'll text you later.

Unknown Number:

Sounds good.

CHAPTER EIGHT

VERONICA

"Okay, Team Sane People: So who do we think it is?" Betty couldn't keep the creeping terror out of her voice. This was the third time she'd circled back to this question, and we were no closer to coming up with any truly solid theories.

You'd think, after living through so many other depraved and violent acts, we "Riverdale youth" (as my mom termed us at the ill-fated time capsule opening) would be all but immune to yet another dead body, especially one that, for the time being, at least, bore little connection to us specifically.

You'd think that, but you'd be wrong.

We were all still processing the grisly contents tucked away inside that maple barrel. In the immediate wake of the discovery, everything happened very quickly. Our parents—ever familiar, it seemed, with elaborate cover-ups and quick-response triages—rushed into action to sweep things back into order as best they could, as quickly as they could. Mom gave some half-hearted rallying cry about how we, as a town, *deserved* an after-party. All I could think then was how she'd said we deserved the time capsule, too. And look at how that had ended up.

Maybe we did *deserve it.*

In any case, the parents were all playing "ignore the stench of rot in the state of Denmark." *Nothing to see here, folks.* Naturally, we weren't buying a moment of it. We knew *way* better than that. In the wake of the ill-conceived after-party, we core four had hunkered down as soon as we were alone and the coast was clear. Right now, La Bonne Nuit was the one place where we could talk freely about what the hell we'd seen—and what the hell to do next.

We were seated, buzzing and alive with dread and morbid curiosity.

"Well, that capsule was buried seventy-five years ago," I said. It was all I had to offer, and it wasn't much.

"Yeah, the body was put in the capsule then, but it was a skeleton, V. Who knows when that person actually died? The bones could have been from any time before that." Betty shuddered.

"In other words, we basically have nothing by way of leads." *And add to that the fact that my very own Mommie Dearest would rather die than pull at this loose thread anymore.* She'd made that abundantly clear.

"I mean, I didn't get that great of a look before my dad hauled me out of there," Jughead said, "and I was pretty freaked out. But from what I did see? It definitely looked bigger. Adult-sized bones."

"It was hard to tell anything from the . . . clothes," Betty ventured. "I mean, it was all pretty tattered. But I'm going to assume female, based on the long hair. And that flowery print."

"Only forensics and DNA testing will tell us for sure," I said, well aware that I sounded uncomfortably similar to a bad crime procedural. "And while my mother assured me— and the rest of the voting public—that she's all over it, I think we can agree she has no plans to approve a deep-dive investigation. No pun intended, but she won't waste any time burying the evidence, as I'm sure I don't have to convince you."

"Sadly, no," Betty said. "Zero convincing necessary."

"Yeah, that tracks. Totally," Jughead said.

"So," I said, sighing, "what fictions did our respective parental figures peddle to us all, respectively? I'll go first: Mom refused to engage and would only tell me that she'd 'take care of it,' whatever the hell *that* means. She's insisting another dead body is strictly NBD, which, I mean, maybe in her world that's actually true? But no less chilling. *'We don't even know that this body—assuming it* is *a human body, and not some sort of tasteless prank—is from Riverdale in the first place.'* She *actually* said that. Like the fact that it was found *in a Riverdale Revels time capsule* wasn't sufficiently convincing."

"That's . . . some high-level self-delusion," Jughead said, arching an eyebrow. "Impressive."

"That's one word for it." I frowned and rubbed my hands up and down my arms. I suddenly had a chill that wouldn't go away. "I mean, is she covering something up about the body, some information? Or does she have *another*, more sinister agenda that requires her full attention, making the body little more than an inconvenience?"

Archie looked at me. "Which would be better?"

I shook my head. "None of the above. I'm certain Daddy's offering to find her a good, thorough cleaner who will make this all go away. Whatever else might be motivating her, she's determined to go through with the Revels, come hell or high water. And an unexpected dead body definitely doesn't fit anywhere up there on her shiny, happy vision board."

"Well, I struck out, too." Jughead punctuated his pronouncement by noisily tearing into a bag of potato chips that I didn't even know we *had* in La Bonne Nuit. He must have had them on him when he came in. For a moment, the room was filled with the sound of aggressive crunching. He swallowed, exaggeratedly, before continuing. "Dad put me off—he was too busy looking around, which, to be fair, made sense. Given he's, you know, the sheriff."

I nodded. "At least one adult is taking this semiseriously. Still, though, if my mom wants this swept under the rug, she'll find a way to make sure that's where it goes. And she'll somehow get your father on board and complicit with her plan. It's what she does."

"He told me not to worry," Jughead said, chuckling slightly to himself at the idea. "He said it with a straight face. As if that were possible. I mean, he always says that. And pretty much always about things that are *definitely* cause for concern."

"He's trying to protect you," Betty said, putting a hand on his knee.

"I wish he wouldn't, though. I mean, sure, I get it. It's what dads are supposed to do. I just wish the adults would realize that it's literally impossible to truly protect us in this town. Being honest would actually be safer, in the long run." He didn't even really sound bitter, just matter-of-fact—which was all the more heartbreaking.

"Honesty. That's a pretty subversive concept around here," Betty said. She rested her chin in her hand.

"Anyway, he assured me he and his team would be looking into it all," Jughead said, skeptical.

"What team?" Betty asked.

"My father's flunkies, no doubt," I fumed. "It stands to reason that my parents would have pounced on the opportunity to bring your father in line with whatever this new dark mystery may be."

Jughead shrugged. "He swore they'd be very 'thorough.'"

"Thorough at *wiping* the place, maybe," Archie said, frustrated. "If that's what Hiram and Hermione want. No offense, Ronnie." His cheeks were red with anger, almost brighter than those ginger locks I so adored.

I waved a hand. "Please, Archiekins. You're preaching to the proverbial choir."

"Yeah, that *wiping* part was kind of implied," Jughead said. "Or if it wasn't explicitly implied, I definitely inferred it. And I don't think I was being presumptuous."

"Well, my dad didn't lie to me or put me off—so, I mean, I guess that's a good thing," Archie said, calm again after his sudden outburst. "But Dad also made it very clear that Mayor Lodge said she would handle it, so he doesn't plan to touch it with a ten-foot pole. Andrews Construction is building the sets for the pageant and doing a bunch of other setup work for the Revels, and he wants to be sure he stays on her good side. We need this gig." He looked guilty, his deep brown eyes sad and soulful.

"At least he was straight with you," Jughead said. "He's in 'see no evil, hear no evil' mode. But he's not, like, just pretending evil completely doesn't exist."

"Yeah. I mean, he was shot. And not too long ago. So I think his days of denying evil are kind of over. That's a pretty hard one to get past." Archie's eyes burned white-hot steel. I knew *he* hadn't gotten past his father's brush with the Black Hood, either.

"Shot, right," Betty said. Her voice rang with guilt and remorse. "By *my* dad. Who, at the very least, is in jail right now, so he hasn't had the chance to lie to me about what the hell is going on." She gave a cynical grin. "There truly is a bright side to everything." The grin faded as quickly as it had appeared. "My mom, on the other hand, is in complete denial. It must be something in the Riverdale water."

"Or the maple syrup," I said, only half kidding. (A quarter.)

"Yeah, and normally, this is the kind of juicy scandal *my* mom would be all over," Betty pointed out. "Especially now that she's at WRIV. It's *extra* shady that she couldn't care less about investigating this. Not for her show. Not for her own curiosity." She tilted her head and held her hands up, the universal gesture for nothing. "She claims she's busy with the Farm. I'm not sure I buy it."

"Betty," Jughead said, low and gentle, "the thing is, she *has* been super wrapped up in that stuff lately. I know it kills you. But . . . I do kind of buy it. Even though I don't like it."

"Ugh, I know you're right," Betty admitted, reluctant. "I guess I'd *rather* she be obsessed with a new body than with the Farm. Potentially the lesser of two evils. Is that twisted?"

"Oh, come now," Jughead said, picking up her hand in his and kissing it. "This is Riverdale. We've basically redefined the meaning of the word 'twisted.' This barely registers on the meter."

"So, what now?" Betty asked, shaking off whatever lingering ennui she was feeling about her mother's most recent weirdness and snapping back into productive mode. "I mean, we have to investigate."

"We do," I said. "But."

"V. There was a *body* in a maple barrel. There can be no 'buts.'"

"There can be one very valid 'but,' which is that our parents told us to leave this alone. And even if we have no intention of doing so—"

"Which we do not," she confirmed, emphatic.

"Even if that's true," I continued smoothly, "or rather, *especially* if that's true, then there needs to be some subterfuge involved. Some low-key attempt to look like we're listening to them. Otherwise they'll be all over us, and in our way, making it infinitely harder to uncover anything."

Betty considered it. "That's actually an excellent point, V," she admitted. "Pretending to behave will keep them off our trail."

"Besides," Archie said, "Veronica and I totally have your back—we'll run point whenever you need us to—but honestly, you and Jug are the sleuths of our group. We all know that. You're the mystery-solving A-team. You guys sniff around, tell us what you find, and give us our marching orders. We'll be in, we promise." He looked at me. "Right?"

"OMG, of course," I said quickly. "We've got your back, total ride-or-die. You know that. But I do think that in the meantime, it would be prudent for Archie and me to go along with our regularly scheduled duties: me coaching Kevin, and whatever else needs doing in the lead-up to the Revels. Archie helping his dad. Plus, we're both official sponsors of the Revels. So we *really* need to play at normalcy. Which, sadly, kind of *is* par for the course for us, around here."

Everyone nodded solemnly at that. It was pretty indisputable.

"We were already covering the whole thing for the *Blue and Gold*," Betty said. "We'll just cover it a little more . . . intensively. And a *lot* less objectively."

"All right, then." Jughead stood, shrugging his Serpents jacket on and pulling his hat down into place. "Ready, Watson?"

"Oh, please," I laughed. "If anything, Betty is the Holmes of your duo."

Betty smiled. "I appreciate the sentiment, V." She stood and slipped into her own powder-pink peacoat. "But if I'm anyone other than Betty Cooper in this scenario, I'm Nancy Drew."

"Touché, B." With the seedlings of a nascent plan in place, we split up. It was time to divide—and, with any luck, conquer.

∿∿∿

Hermione Lodge:

Hi. Just checking in to be sure we're on track for the pageant set construction to begin tomorrow morning?

Fred Andrews:

8 a.m. sharp.

Hermione Lodge:

And there won't be any issues, given what happened at today's ceremony?

Fred Andrews:

None on my end. You'll let me know if anything comes up for you?

Hermione Lodge:

Of course. We're investigating the issue as we speak. And I appreciate your discretion. Perhaps we can find some room in the budget to improve your fee.

Fred Andrews:

Not necessary, Madam Mayor, but I'm not too proud to accept. Gratefully.

Hermione Lodge:

Of course. Everyone in Riverdale is just so impressed with your dedication to our hometown.

Fred Andrews:

What can I say? Our hometown is my home.

ᴧᴧᴧ

Hermione Lodge:

Alice, I hope you don't mind my being in touch. With regards to the . . . wrinkle we experienced at the time capsule opening earlier this evening.

Alice Cooper:

"Wrinkle"—is that what we're calling it? Spectacular.

Hermione Lodge:

Well, Alice, that's why I'm reaching out. To be completely honest, we don't know WHAT to call it just yet. Which is why I think it would be downright inappropriate if you were to report on the event before we have a full understanding of the situation.

Alice Cooper:

Until you have your ducks in a row, you mean. Relax, Madam Mayor. Believe it or not, for once, I couldn't care less about the latest scandal to plague this godforsaken town. I've got other things to worry about.

Hermione Lodge:

Do I even want to ask?

Alice Cooper:

When have you ever? Don't worry your pretty little head about it, Hermione.

TUESDAY

CHAPTER NINE

From the Office of Mayor Hermione Lodge

To the citizens of Riverdale:

All of us at Town Hall wish to apologize again for the unfortunate incident at last night's time capsule opening. Needless to say, it came as a surprise to us all. We hope no one experienced any excessive distress and that you're all still enthusiastic about the upcoming Revels celebrations. We have so many wonderful events in store!

The Revels has events for all ages! From tonight's pet parade to tomorrow's bingo night, we hope to see Riverdale citizens young and old enjoying this week's entertainment. And we especially hope to see you all dressed up at Friday's elegant Cocktails and Canapés, where we'll have a chance to sample some delicious snacks, courtesy of Pop Tate's own Chock'Lit Shoppe and other local vendors. Bring your appetites!

Most important, however, I write to set your mind at ease regarding the bones found in the time capsule barrel. Our coroner's office has confirmed that they are in fact not authentic remains. It seems we've all fallen victim to a harmless—albeit incredibly juvenile—prank. And while that may be disappointing, hopefully the certainty and closure brings with it a good amount of peace.

We'll be looking into the origins of the prank and will keep you all posted. In the meantime, please do feel free to reach out with any questions you may have.

Sincerely,
Hermione Lodge

Veronica:

Bravo, Mom. I can't begin to imagine what your endgame is here, with metaphorically burying the bones in the time capsule, but it looks like you've gotten what you wanted. I suppose I shouldn't be surprised.

Hermione Lodge:

Mija, despite the fact that I owe you zero explanations, I'd be happy to show you Curdle Jr.'s report myself. Until then, I strongly suggest you reconsider how you speak to your mother.

Veronica:

Believe me, I've given it plenty of consideration.

~~~

Hermione Lodge:

I have the reports. Everything's perfect. Thanks for taking care of this.

Hiram Lodge:

I promised you, didn't I, mi amor?

~~~

Hot Dog's good to go and ready for his close up? Jughead told me to check in.

Sweet Pea:

Uh, yeah, MOM. I think I got it.

Sweet Pea:

The dog's been washed and brushed and looking forward to his moment in the spotlight.

Sweet Pea:

Fangs even got him a new leash for the occasion.

Toni:

Perf. I'll take lots of pics.

Sweet Pea:

Tell me you haven't started an Instagram. Not exactly Serpent-style.

Toni:

I haven't . . . but I kinda LOVE that idea.

∿∿∿

JUGHEAD

In the absence of a single, solitary lead on the body in the maple barrel (only in Riverdale, my friends, only in Riverdale), Betty and I figured the next best thing to do would be to start by going straight to . . . well, if not necessarily *the* source, then *a* source at least: Pop Tate, a man whose persona embodied the soul of our town more than maybe any other of our founding families.

Besides—he was the one who'd given Archie's dad the map for excavating the time capsule in the first place. Institutional knowledge was a powerful thing.

Pop seemed to know a little bit about *everything*, particularly when it came to Riverdale, and Betty and I were hoping that this would be as true of the time capsule, and the history of the Revels, as it was for anything else.

Betty had study hall during third period, and I had English, which I was doing well enough in that I felt okay ducking out just this once, in the name of something inarguably more important.

"Besides," I told Betty, "we were *assigned* the job of covering the Revels for the *Blue and Gold* by Principal Weatherbee himself. Isn't this just an extension of that, really? Which means that it's essentially a school project. And since it's journalism, I think it's basically just another form of English class."

"Wow, Jug," Betty said, feigning at impressed. "Well done. And here we thought Hermione Lodge was the one who was good with spin."

"Not bad, right? I try."

We had just parked my motorcycle and were standing outside Pop's, contemplative. "This is only a recon mission, Juggie," Betty said, tightening her ponytail and fixing her gaze.

"Yep," I said, taking her hand. "Let's go fishing."

Inside, it was quiet—a few cars in the driveway and some booths filled with retirees grabbing a late breakfast. Pop registered our arrival with an inscrutable look, like he'd been expecting it, yes, but he wasn't sure whether he was happy about it. Generally speaking, Pop seemed to think Betty and I were determined to get ourselves killed, the way we insisted on poking our noses anywhere things didn't smell quite right in Riverdale. And maybe he was right. We'd sure come close enough, plenty of times.

"Hey, Pop," I said, giving him my best "winning" smile.

"Jughead and Betty. Please tell me you're here for a milk shake and some fries."

"Pop, it's ten fifteen in the morning," Betty said.

"Which, normally, is the perfect time for a burger, Pop. And believe me, I'd never want to say no to an offer like that. But alas, as I'm sure you suspect, based on the look on your face, we've got some other fish to fry right now." I stepped in to clarify the purpose of our visit, but even as I declined the offer of food, my stomach gave a grumble. I glanced at Betty. "I mean . . . we can fry fish *and* drink a milk shake, right?"

She grinned. "I'm still full from breakfast, Jug—but I know *you* can."

"Other fish to fry, huh?" Pop asked as he moved to get started on my milk shake. Betty and I settled ourselves in at the counter.

"Or rather, other maple barrels to tap," Betty quipped. Her expression, though, belied her playful tone. "Specifically, bone-stuffed barrels connected to a tradition that was apparently near and dear to this town's settlers—and yet, is somehow missing from the pages of every local history book."

My girl liked to get straight to the point. It was one of my many favorite things about her.

"Are you kids *sure* you can't find some other way to have fun?" Pop asked, shaking his head. His tone was light, but I knew he was worried.

"Pop, you know you love us just the way we are," I said. "This *is* how we have fun."

He sighed and began to wipe down the counter. "You kids—you're asking for trouble. If the mayor says the barrel was a prank, why can't you believe it?"

"Because it would be the most random prank ever. Because fake dead bodies in a town that has an unexpectedly high body count aren't funny. Because supposedly the Revels were this whole big thing, like, forever, but not even Cheryl Blossom—who knows everything about Riverdale's history—has ever heard of them." Betty ticked her reasons off on her fingers as she listed them.

I nodded, patting her on the shoulder. "I think that about covers it."

Pop took a deep breath. He leaned forward on the counter, looking right at us. "Okay," he started. "So let's say you're right. Let's say it *wasn't* a prank. No one knows who it is or even how old the body is. No clue. And meanwhile, the coroner himself is calling it a fake. The mayor has the report."

I winced. He made a point. "She did flat-out offer Veronica a look at them."

"You know that doesn't necessarily mean anything. Maybe she forged them," Betty countered. "Or had someone else forge them for her. Maybe she's calling Veronica's bluff."

"Okay. But *why*?" I persisted, playing devil's advocate. "*If* those bones are real—Betty, you saw them. You know the condition they were in. If they *are* real, whoever that was in the barrel is *long* dead. What the hell would they have to do with Hermione?"

Betty looked at me. "I have no idea," she admitted. "But still, something doesn't add up."

"Why does no one in this town understand that the best

thing to do when a dead body is discovered is to get as far away from it and whatever made it dead as you possibly can?" Pop sounded exasperated.

"Because we've learned that the secrets that people keep in this town literally kill," I said.

"And because in this town, that's impossible to do," Betty added. "Pop, you should know as well as anyone. The Black Hood shot Fred Andrews *right here*. You mopped up the blood yourself."

Pop took this in, his face growing even more grave, if that were even possible. I couldn't say what was going on in his head, but he seemed to be coming to a decision of some kind. "You two *really* don't believe that it was a prank?"

"I don't," Betty said. "We don't."

"It *is* extremely suspicious," I agreed.

"And you don't have any leads?"

"You were our first stop. You always know everything about the history of this town—even the things Cheryl somehow misses. Didn't you tell me once about how you served *Madonna* and her entourage in that booth there"—I pointed—"back in the eighties?"

He smiled. "Might have."

"Exactly."

Betty's eyes lit up. "And you and FP! Just yesterday you were talking about how some of our parents—or, you know some adults, anyway—were eager to bring back the Revels. Even though it seemed as though no one even knew about the Revels in the first place."

"Betty," Pop said, slow and measured, "if *no one* knew about the Revels, how did anyone know to bring them back?" He peered at her and then turned away, walking toward a corner booth with a fresh-brewed pot of coffee.

"He's right. *Someone* knew. Maybe a few someones." Betty looked at me. "We have to figure out who it was—who lobbied to reinstate the Revels. Can we ask your dad?"

I shook my head emphatically. "That's a nonstarter. As soon as he got the word from Mayor Lodge this morning, he told me: That's their story, and they're sticking to it. Even if there is some massive cover-up going on, we're not going to get anything else about the Revels from him."

"Pop's right, though," Betty insisted. "*Someone* knew *something*. I think we just have to dig deeper."

I looked at her. "Anything on file about the town history would be at the library."

"Well, then, I guess that should be our next stop," Betty said, decisive.

Pop looked satisfied as he came back to the counter. "I suppose that's where I'd go, too. But *after* school," he added knowingly.

I put down some money for my milk shake, and Betty and I hopped down from our stools. "Then I suppose that's where we'll go," I said. "*After* school, of course."

We were so caught up in the possibility of a new lead that when we stepped out the door of the diner, we immediately collided with a tangle of limbs and catering trays.

"Oh god—we're so sorry—" Betty started. She cut off abruptly when she realized who was holding the tower of aluminum in her outstretched arms. "Evelyn?" She got cooler and pulled back just the slightest bit.

There was no love lost between the two girls, and I didn't blame Betty one bit.

But why was Evelyn here, now, in the middle of the school day, carrying a metric ton of aluminum trays in her scrawny arms?

"Big party at the Farm?" Betty asked, raising an eyebrow. "Getting some Pop's takeout? Given how much you guys like sharing chores and stuff, I would've thought you'd do all the cooking together."

Evelyn gave Betty a small, patient smile. "You're right at that, Betty. We do generally prepare all our meals together. Cooking is such a wonderful way to build a sense of community, after all. But this is for the Revels. We're helping Pop prepare canapés. You know, for Cocktails and Canapés on Friday? A few of us Farmies volunteered to help with the event. Transporting supplies, working as sous-chefs, setting up on the day of. You know, that sort of thing. I was just dropping these trays off for Pop. So we have them when the food prep is done."

"*Really.*" Betty looked suspicious. (It did sound remarkably mainstream for a group that seemed to vastly prefer social fringes and secrecy.)

"Of course." Evelyn flashed a smug, quick grin. "Our family shares everything, you know. There are no secrets."

"Of course," Betty said, her voice thin and reedy. "I remember."

I wrapped an arm around Betty's waist. I could see her hands clenching, forming tight fists that were so intense her fingernails would dig bloody crescents into her palms. I needed to get her away, and fast.

Leave it to Evelyn to be just that weird, doing nothing more than carrying catering trays.

Randomly, in the middle of a school day.

We could deal with the Farm—and Betty's mom and sister's relationship to them—another day. Somehow, I was sure we'd have plenty more chances.

"See you around, Evelyn," I said. "Good luck, you know, sous-ing." I threw her a wave over my shoulder as I guided Betty away. Maybe there was time to try to calm down a little, before we got back to school.

Delusion: In Riverdale, we all practiced it, sooner or later.

First thing you learn is the Maple Man.

And that's not a story, either, or a code or a symbol for anything deeper. No, the Maple Man is real, and he's coming for your daughters. Your sisters. Your girls. The young ones. Innocent, you know?

Those girls. That's what makes the maple syrup flow.

They made a pageant of it. Young girls lined up, who would be the lucky one? Being selected—that was a great honor. And the town thrived.

People like to say that Riverdale was built on maple syrup. But we know better. The Maple Man knows better.

Riverdale was built on blood.

It probably won't be too much longer now. Before the truth comes out. Before it can't be denied any longer. Before folks will have to own another horror, another reality.

I wonder: Will I be relieved, when it's all over? I think I might be.

But for now, mostly—I'm just afraid.

CHAPTER TEN

Dr. Curdle Jr.:

Have you had a chance to review both of the documents I sent along, Madam Mayor?

Hermione Lodge:

Yes, and thank you for those. As you saw, I passed the information about the prank along in a Town Hall memo. I trust you received your cash donation?

Dr. Curdle Jr.:

Indeed. I saw. It was quite well worded.

Dr. Curdle Jr.:

And the donation arrived without trouble. Thank you.

Hermione Lodge:

It's the least we can do. But I wanted to confirm: According to the second report, you're saying there's no possible way to identify the victim based on the bones?

Dr. Curdle Jr.:

Correct. They're too old and too deteriorated, unfortunately. All I can tell is they were human.

Hermione Lodge:

I see. Well, thank you again. We appreciate your swift . . . compliance.

Dr. Curdle Jr.:

Of course, Madam Mayor. And I appreciate your charitable support.

⌒⌒⌒

Hermione Lodge:

Curdle has his marching orders. I think this is all sewn up.

Hiram Lodge:

Glad to hear it. Let me know if there's anything else.

⌒⌒⌒

ARCHIE

Veronica had asked me to meet her after school, though she didn't say exactly why. Betty and Jughead were off investigating the maple barrel case—they were going to do some research at the library, they said. Meanwhile, Veronica and I were supposed to be keeping up appearances, since our parents were demanding that everyone carry on, post body-in-the-time-capsule, as though it were just another day in Riverdale.

(Which, in some ways, it was. Just, you know, not the way they wanted it to be.)

Anyway, from what I could tell, there were about a million things going on, all important, a bunch seeming to contradict one another. The best I could think to do was just go where I was told and do what was asked of me, as best I could. So here I was, pulling the jalopy up in front of Kevin's house, wondering when the last time was that I'd been here and coming up blank. Ronnie'd done a few sleepovers with him, and there was that cast party he threw last year before the school play . . . but other than that, as much as I liked Kevin, we didn't tend to hang out one-on-one, without Ronnie or Betty around. Had it been that long? Maybe.

He looked happy to see me when he opened the door. His face was a little red and sweaty, and he was wearing a very fitted black T-shirt with black leggings.

"Hey, Arch! Veronica's downstairs. Do you want something to drink?" He pulled me inside without any explanation of his outfit or what might be going on. I decided to just go with it.

"Sure, a soda'd be great, if you have one," I said.

"Yep. Of course."

We took a quick detour to the kitchen and grabbed some sodas from the fridge.

"And a Pellegrino for Veronica, I got those special, at her request, I guess it's the RROTC Scout in me—very dependable," Kevin said, then headed down into the basement, which I vaguely remembered from that party. Of course, it looked pretty different when it wasn't stuffed to the brim with kids stumbling and waving blue and red Solo cups all over.

The soundtrack was different today, too.

"Is that . . . *Cats* you guys are playing?" I didn't know much about show tunes, but I dimly recalled this one from an elementary school trip to a Riverdale Playhouse production, back around third or fourth grade. It made an impression, especially being one of the only musicals I'd ever seen.

(None of us knew that the cats were going to jump out into the audience, and Betty, who was sitting next to me like always, totally freaked when it happened. She shrieked and grabbed my arm so hard I had finger-shaped bruises where her hands had been for a week. I thought for sure we'd get kicked out, but I guess these places are used to big groups of little kids. No one even blinked, and eventually, Betty was able to chill out.)

I rounded the corner to see Veronica in a pair of black tights and a black leotard. She had dance shoes on, too. Between her and Kevin, the overall effect was pretty professional.

"Archiekins!" She ran up and kissed me. Her face was slick with a light sheen of sweat, and pinkish, too.

"You guys are . . . dancing. To *Cats*?" It was literally the last thing I'd expected to see, coming down these stairs. Even though, looking at the two of them in their quasi uniforms, it kind of fit.

"OMG, Kev, you're a lifesaver," she said, twisting the cap off the Pellegrino bottle he passed her. It gave a little hiss as the metal seal broke. "How did you know?"

"Call it gay husband's intuition," he said, popping the top to his own soda and then mine, which he passed to me.

"Everyone needs one of those," Veronica proclaimed, then raised her bottle. "A toast. To friends."

"To friends," I said, clinking my can against their drinks. We took a sip.

Veronica swallowed, pressing the cool glass against her forehead. "Divine." She fanned herself for a minute, then looked at me. "And to answer your question: Yes, Archiekins, that is *Cats* that you're hearing."

"Okay," I said slowly. "But . . . why?"

"Just a little something Kevin and I are cooking up for the talent portion of the Royal Maple pageant."

"Veronica, you definitely live a charmed life," Kevin said, grinning. "The perfectly doting gay husband *and* a sensitive yet hunky boyfriend who recognizes show tunes when he hears them?"

"Don't forget the ride-or-die bestie who murders the Bechdel test *and* practices Vixens routines with me after school. It's true. This is the postmillennial version of having it all, and I make no apologies." She set down her drink and twisted her hair into a ponytail, grinning with satisfaction.

"Okay," she said, "so here's the twist: For Kevin's talent, we're actually going to perform a dance together."

"Can you do that?" I asked. "Even if you're not actually in the pageant?"

She nodded. "We spoke to Weatherbee, who gave us his blessing. The judges will know to evaluate Kevin based on his performance, not mine." She shot him a sidelong glance. "Which is a shame for you, Kev, because Isadora Duncan had nothing on me."

"I would happily take the point boost, but it's not up to me," Kevin said. "But I'm sure Archie is dying to know why we asked him to come by."

"I am curious," I admitted. "Not that I'm not happy to see you both."

"Likewise, Archie," Veronica said. "The thing is, we need an outside opinion, and we were hoping you could provide it. It's about music, and of course, *you're* a musician."

"Who knows musical theater," Kevin put in. "The question being, can you give objective feedback *despite* your relationship with Veronica?"

I laughed. "Sure. Hit me."

"We're having a bit of an artistic debate about our choice of song for our performance."

"Not *Cats*, then?"

"Maybe *Cats*," Kevin interjected. "That's part of the artistic debate. Most of the debate, that is."

"That's the debate," Veronica clarified.

"Creative differences?" I asked.

"Well, Archiekins, here's the rub," Veronica said, laying it down. "Given the sheer number of River Vixens and former Pussycats who've signed up for the Royal Maple pageant—"

"Still loving that gender-nonspecific title," Kevin mused, interrupting.

"That's the one thing they did right," Veronica agreed. "But anyway, the vast preponderance of people we know who are participating in the pageant are singers or dancers. So we wanted to perform something that would set us apart. Show tunes seemed like a good fit and safe choice as far as being unique was concerned."

"Okay, so what's the debate part of this debate?" I asked.

"Veronica suggested something like a Janet Jackson–esque take on 'My Shot,' from *Hamilton*." He waited a beat to see if I recognized the mention, but all I know about *Hamilton* is that it basically has a legion of superfans and the tickets cost a ton. Seeing my blank expression, Kevin went on. "Hip-hop with lots of pops and flourishes, maybe chairs for props."

"That could be cool," I said.

"It absolutely could be. And I cannot *tell* you how many times I've watched the show in twenty-minute increments on ViewTube." His eyes narrowed. "That ticket lottery is such a tease. There are legit military torture tactics that are more humane."

"You've been waiting on lottery tickets?" Veronica looked genuinely stunned. "Kev, I can't believe you didn't say anything! Daddy and Lin know each other from their benefit to raise money for Shakespeare in the Park. I'll make a phone call. Fret no more, friend."

Kevin's eyes gleamed. "Veronica, so help me, if you are joking with me, this marriage is off."

She waved a hand at him. "Remind me tonight." She took a breath and returned to the issue at hand. "Anyway. Kevin agrees that it *could* be cool. But the thing is, it probably won't stand out as much as it could. I mean, for every Toni, Ginger, and Tina at Riverdale High, there's a Nicki, Beyoncé, or Ariana—with a top song in heaviest rotation and a signature dance to accompany it. And how would that really be different, stylistically, from what we would be planning to do?"

"Veronica!" Kevin gasped. "You know Queen Bey is always mentioned first when presenting a list of pop icons. It's in the *Chicago Manual of Style*, right after the section on the serial comma."

"Fair. With apologies to Her Highness. *So*"—she brushed back a stray lock of hair that had escaped from her ponytail and into her eyes—"Kevin's countersuggestion was something slow, traditional—a ballroom dance we could do as a waltz. Hence, 'Memory.'"

"Hence, 'Memory,'" I agreed. "I see where you're going, with the logic, I mean."

"But Veronica's not sure it's the right choice." Kevin sighed.

"It's a little cheesy," she said. "And technically, it's not really a waltz-type song, either. So it's not the most organic choice. That's all I said. It wasn't a definitive *yea* or *nay* vote."

"It's *definitely* a little cheesy," Kevin agreed. "But can we at least acknowledge the elephant in the room? Let's be real, guys: *Musical theater* is a little cheesy. That's, like, its whole thing. Let there be no pretense. And *Cats* is a classic, and there's a reason for that. I, for one, think we should just embrace it."

"He makes a solid point," I said. "Also very logical."

"I *know*," Veronica said, pouting. "That's just it. I don't generally disagree. I'm just not totally sold yet. It doesn't . . . I don't know, stir my soul, or whatever."

"*Stir your soul?*" Kevin echoed, doubtful. "That's a pretty tall order for the song selection in a local beauty pageant's talent show portion," he pointed out. "*Your* soul, specifically, has gone to the Parrot Cay wellness retreat in Turks and Caicos—*multiple* times, I might add—and done yoga alongside the likes of Demi Moore and Karlie Kloss. It is not easily stirred by lesser experiences. Plus you're not even competing!"

"Mmm," she said. "The Ayurvedic scalp massage was pretty life changing, too. Remind me to book us one of *those* after I score those *Hamilton* tickets. That would be mental note number two. But, yes, point taken."

"When do you have to submit your music to the pageant people?" I asked, thinking about solutions.

"Not until Friday," Veronica said. "And TBH, I'm sure they'd let us sneak something in Saturday morning. I mean, not to fall back on anything so mundanely unappealing as blatant nepotism, but I *am* the mayor's daughter. They'll probably float us a few extra hours if we need it."

"But the choreography would be different, if we went with 'My Shot,'" Kevin pointed out. "So we don't actually have until Friday."

"Right. So, flip to decide—ballad or hip-hop? And, you

know, your choices aren't *only* Cats or *Hamilton*. If 'Memory' isn't right, there's definitely another ballad, something better that will come to you."

"Flip a coin," Veronica mused. "Could it really be so simple?"

"I'm in," Kevin said. "Otherwise, we're just at an impasse."

Veronica smiled. "That's the unfortunate downside of a partnership between two strong-willed, confident individuals. Our crosses to bear."

"True."

There was a small, comfortable-looking couch in a well-worn plaid pushed against the wall, and I settled into it now, bringing my soda with me. "Show me what you've got," I suggested. "I want to see it, before you flip. And then we can take it from there."

"Fresh eyes! Perfect, Archiekins!" Veronica held Kevin's phone out to him. "Maestro, cue it up."

CHAPTER ELEVEN

Sweet Pea:

You around?

Josie:

What's up?

Sweet Pea:

Just wondering if you wanted to chill tonight.

Josie:

Aw, thanks, but I can't. Motorcade and Music is on Thursday, I've gotta practice.

Sweet Pea:

All work and no play . . .

Josie:

Keeps this diva on top.

JOSIE

I'd been in my room with noise-canceling headphones on when Sweet Pea texted. True to his semi-ironic Serpent name, homeboy really was a sweetie, but he just didn't seem to get that I really wanted to keep our thing—whatever it was, or had been—low-key and under wraps.

Did I like him? Totally. And kissing him was not remotely a chore. But I was emphatically *not* in the market for a boyfriend right now. Yeah, I was lonely. But Juilliard was right there, floating out on the not-at-all-distant horizon like some kind of glittery mirage plucked straight from my wildest fantasies. Juilliard was the best, the absolute number one place to be, if I was seriously going to do this pop star, music thing. Which I was. I *already* was, really. Because *I'm* the best, too.

And sometimes being the best? Means making sacrifices.

I knew that all too well.

Another thing I knew? Connections—friends, boyfriends, people you might open your heart to, that you'd want to trust? Those don't come easy. I've been burned, and it hurt. No matter how good I was at hiding that. When it comes to connections, I'd basically stopped trying to make them.

So, yeah—Sweet Pea and I were texting, and it was fine. But I was too busy to make time for him. And more than that, I was in a funk, and talking to him just now only served to remind me that I *was* in a funk.

I put my headphones down. Forget practice, forget thinking about the stupid motorcade. I stood up, stretched my arms overhead, and headed down to the kitchen to grab something to drink.

"Josie!"

I almost shrieked, I was so surprised. I jumped back and slammed the refrigerator door shut, spilling some of the soda I'd just poured onto my shirt. It was cold and sticky. "Perfect." Add a load of laundry to this evening's roster and it was looking lit AF.

I turned to see Archie Andrews standing in the doorway, looking amused and also a little guilty. But not *that* guilty.

"Sorry, I didn't mean to startle you," he said. He grabbed a handful of paper towels from the counter and wet them at the sink, then clumsily went to dab where the soda was soaking through my clothes, pulling back when he realized, awkwardly, that he was basically making an inadvertent grab for my chest.

He was so close to me I could smell whatever shampoo he used—grassy and fresh. For a second, goose pimples broke out on my arms. And *that* startled me even more than his coming up behind me in the kitchen, the way the sudden nearness caused a tiny involuntary reaction in me. I pulled away, grabbed my own paper towel, and started scrubbing my shirt—a little too intensely, like in a Lady Macbeth kind of way.

"It's fine, Archie. Nothing a little time in the gentle cycle can't solve." I sighed.

Lit. AF. "Much simpler than most of my other problems."

I swear I wasn't fishing for a reaction; if you'd asked me whether I thought opening up to Archie Andrews was a good idea, I would have said you were insane. As I think I've established, I didn't really think opening up to anyone was a good idea. It just came out. Long day.

(Week.)

(Month.)

(High school career?)

His forehead immediately crinkled with concern. "What's up?"

I waved him off. "It's fine," I said. "Seriously. Don't worry about it. What are you doing here, anyway?" Then I remembered. "Oh, Veronica's with Kevin, right? I heard them disappear downstairs. And—sorry, that sounded aggressive, instead of curious." I smiled, trying to give him a little more softness. *Why was my default always so defensive?*

"No worries," Archie said. "Yeah, they're practicing for the talent portion. Ballroom dance, I guess. Veronica got approved to perform with Kevin even though she's not officially competing."

"That's fun!"

"Yeah, Ronnie wanted me to come by so I could see their dance, give some opinion on their musical selection—"

"They wanted *your* opinion on the music?" I couldn't help it; I'd blurted it out like an involuntary muscle spasm, something completely beyond my control.

I blushed. "Sorry. I didn't mean—I mean, you know I think you've got big talent, Archie, it's just—" I sighed. "I should probably just quit with the whole talking thing while I'm . . . not at all ahead. I'm gonna choke on my own foot if this keeps up."

"No, no, I get it," he insisted, cutting me off. "I mean, obviously you're Riverdale High's resident rock star. I don't think there's anyone around who'd argue that."

"Well, it's sweet that she's so invested in helping Kevin," I said, my tone going low and wistful for a hot minute. "Must be nice." The words were out before I could think about it, much less bite my tongue. *WTH, Josie—what's the deal with the self-pity party?*

"Yeah." He ran a hand through that thicket of red hair, leaving it sticking up in fifteen different directions. It made him look young, sweet, like a little kid. "You're not doing the pageant, right?"

"No, sir," I told him. "I'm one and done—all about the Motorcade and Music on Thursday night."

"Oh, right! You're singing, of course."

"All by my lonesome," I confirmed, unable to resist. Another stab of self-pity poked at my ribs.

"Why lonesome? I thought you deliberately struck out on your own this year."

I knew he meant *struck out on your own* as in: charted your own course. But it was still hard to hear it as anything other than *struck out—all on your own.*

"That I did," I said, swallowing hard.

He tilted his head, looked at me with new understanding dawning. "And things have been weird with the Pussycats ever since."

I shrugged. "I get it. They felt betrayed. Rejected. Hell, it *was* rejection, of a kind."

"Yeah, that stuff's always hard," he said, the look in his eyes saying he meant it, like he knew what he was talking about. "I got a lot of grief when I started to work more seriously on my music and didn't have as much time for football. The guys definitely didn't understand."

I gave him a small smile. "You mean Reggie Mantle somehow lacked the nuanced emotional intelligence to make you feel comfortable with your choice?"

"Yeah." Archie laughed. "Shocker." Then he cocked his head, like he'd had a small aha moment. "Hey," he started. "So, if your—brother?"

"Sure. 'Brother' works," I said. "We're still easing into it all."

"Right. So, if your brother and my girlfriend are gonna perform together, what if we . . . joined forces, too?"

Later, when I replayed the little interaction with Archie in the kitchen, it seemed almost foregone that we'd come to this conclusion. It made sense: We'd played together before, we knew we were good together, and while neither of us was exactly shy about performing live, we were both nursing some mega-vulnerability. In retrospect, it was funny that it even took us as long as it did to bring the conversation around that way.

In the moment, though, Archie managed to take me by surprise. Maybe it was a mix of things, not the least being how I was still reeling from the on-off thing with Sweet Pea, the brush-off from my 'Cats, and the vague sense of random, illogical FOMO about hearing that Kevin had asked *Veronica* to team up with him for the pageant. Just one of those weird, insecure human moments, I guess. Any port in a storm, that kind of thing.

But a tiny part of me wondered if it was more than that, somehow. Archie was endearing, hard to resist. Like, not in a romantic way—he was with Veronica, and I'm *so* not that girl—but just kind of that "nice boy" thing your mom told you about. Sunny vibes that were appealing, especially when so many other things in your life felt a little stormier.

Archie had seen his share of storms, of course. But that essence of him, that quintessential "Archie-ness," was still there, skating just below the surface. It was infectious, even for a cynic like me.

So when he suggested it—teaming up, maybe even performing an original collaboration, if we could get it together in time—I *was* totally surprised. Turns out I'd been in serious wallow mode, and a sunny lifeline was entirely unexpected.

Being as I'm no fool, I said yes. We agreed to meet at lunch the next day to put together a short set. You've gotta take the sunshine where it comes.

Veronica:

Hey! So, went over to Kev's to practice his talent piece for the pageant.

Betty:

Ballroom?

Veronica:

Ballroom. We flipped, and the odds were not in my favor. Yours truly will be doing her best unironic Ginger Rogers to CATS. Promise me you'll have any video evidence destroyed.

Betty:

Swearsies. And Archie came by?

Veronica:

Yup. The coin flip was his idea, actually. So. Oh! And he's gonna perform with Josie at the Motorcade kickoff thing. They talked when he came by.

Betty:

Fun!

Veronica:

I know, I'm glad he's getting a chance to perform instead of only working behind the scenes.

Betty:

And YOU'RE having fun, too?

Veronica:

OMG, SO much. I know I was cranky about the pageant and it having all those sexist roots, but I've gotta admit . . . I'm kind of getting into it. Being Kevin's stage mom is a fun gig.

Betty:

How could it not be? As long as you keep him on the straight and narrow, avoid a whole Lohan-style flameout, I think you're good.

Veronica:

Will do.

Veronica:

How goes the sleuthing?

Betty:

Still very much in progress. Give me a little more time.

Veronica:

Always. I've got faith in my girl. Keep me posted! 💋

Betty:

👋 TTYL!

CHAPTER TWELVE

Chuck:

Yo, dawg.

Reggie:

What up?

Chuck:

You figured out what you're gonna do for the talent thing yet?

Reggie:

Other than flex? Ha ha.

Chuck:

Well, I was thinking kind of along those lines. I know Keller's doing some dance WITH Veronica. So what if we did something together, too? Like, since partners are allowed?

Reggie:

I mean, no offense, I'm totally open-minded and stuff, man, but I'm not really trying to be waltzing around onstage with you, literally.

Reggie:

Also, I think Ronnie's only helping Kevin because she isn't actually in the pageant.

Chuck:

Uh, yeah. I meant spar, bro. But, good point.

Reggie:

Sorry to disappoint, bud. It's every man for himself in this thing and you're gonna be eating my dust.

Chuck:

You wish, Mantle.

⌢⌢⌢

BETTY

Dear Diary:

The final bell had barely started ringing before Juggie and I were out the door to continue our investigation. (Skipping school was not on the menu if we were trying to "act normal," whatever that means.)

Like so much of the town itself, on the surface, the Riverdale Public Library <u>appeared</u> charming enough. It was a sweet-looking white clapboard building with a well-tended flower patch in its front garden that was thriving impressively, even as the fall weather crept over us. It was a welcoming building, even though the business that brought us here was hardly warm and fuzzy.

We'd been there since school ended, several hours, by now. Long enough that we were bleary from the dim fluorescent lighting overhead and dizzy from slide after slide of microfiche. Normally I love the library, but today all the dead ends were stressing me out.

"I don't get it, Jug," I said, pushing away from the carrel and blinking. The photonegative images from the microfiche film danced on the insides of my eyelids. "The Revels were supposed to have been around for generations before the town's founding. But there's legit no mention of them in any of these records."

"Sadly, that seems to be the conclusion to draw." He had dragged a chair to my carrel, where the projector was, and we were staggered unevenly in the small space. The projector rested beside a looming desktop computer, and the entire expanse of the carrel was cluttered. It was really only intended for one person. I didn't mind having him close, of course (who are we kidding? I loved having him close), but this was snug, and I was starting to feel restless, having nothing to do with Jughead. The investigation was making me twitchy. The investigation, and the lack of viable leads.

"Right. So the question is, why?" I groaned, totally exhausted and completely frustrated. The town had generations of history preserved on these films: weddings, graduations, county fairs...It even had a subsection of agrarian weather reports taken from the Farmers' Almanac. We could literally access the change of precipitation from a specific date a half century ago. The materials seemed to uniformly be dated back to the 1860s. The smallest, most everyday details were available in the film, apparently.

But no mention of the Revels.

"I think the real question we should be asking is, why has Librarian Dinkle refused to embrace the digital age?" Jughead shot the perky, gray-haired woman behind the reference desk an uneasy smile to show he was kidding (sort of), but she hadn't heard him. "I'm all for retro appeal, you know that, but this search would have gone a lot faster with a little 'control F' action."

I rolled my eyes. "Jughead. This is Riverdale. The town that time forgot. Does anyone here have <u>any</u> idea what decade it actually is?"

"Fair enough," he admitted, grinning. "And it works in my favor when the 'retro' extends to Pop's menu prices."

"Exactly," I told him. "Now shush. The problem we're having isn't the medium of these Revels articles—the problem is their lack of existence in the first place."

"Okay," Jughead said, a new determination lighting up his face. "So what do we know?"

"The time capsule was buried at the original founding of Riverdale, in 1941."

"Well, if the adults and authority figures in this town are to be believed, then yes," Jug said. "Which, frankly, I'm not convinced that they are. Who knows <u>when and where</u> the time capsule might have actually come from in the first place?"

"I hear you," I said, rubbing my fingers along my hairline, where my ponytail was pulled so tight I was starting to get a headache. (Or maybe that was just the investigation?) "But logically, the town burying a time capsule at the time of the founding makes a lot of sense. Definitely more sense than someone digging it up seventy-five years later and putting a fake body inside as a prank. So I think it makes sense to operate on the assumption that what we know about the time capsule itself is the truth. Even if we're, you know, keeping an open mind."

"My mind is so open I'm starting to think my brains might be leaking out," Jug said, kidding, but not really. I swatted him, trying to get him to focus. "No, but seriously," he said, settling into his seat to show me just how incredibly serious he was. (It semi-worked.) "Maybe we should fine-tune the search. Instead of trying to dig up articles on the Revels, why not just look up specific events? Who knows—maybe the name wasn't formalized right away, or there's something else, some other reason why the event wouldn't show up in a search."

"So we should be looking for something else. A different search."

Were there even any different searches left? We'd tried a bunch of keyword combinations, along with some other sort of backdoor attempts to find intel about the Revels, but we were still coming up empty. It was like banging our heads against a wall but marginally less fun. "We've tried 'Revels,' and we've tried 'mayors.' We've tried specific mayors' names."

"Also 'time capsules.'" Jughead drummed his fingers on the tabletop. "Ah! But funnily enough, we didn't find anything about 'time capsules of death' in the papers. Which is a shame, because it's such a catchy phrase. Feels like a real lost opportunity."

I couldn't help but smile at that. "Riverdale sure does like to bury its skeletons deep in the closet," I agreed.

"Or, at the very least, wrap them up in something sweet, like a maple syrup barrel," Jughead added. "In this case rather literally."

"And then gloss the whole thing over with a shiny-pretty celebration..."

"Like the Revels," Jug said, making a patient but undeniable "Yes, haven't we covered this?" face.

"Like the _pageant_," I corrected him.

"The Royal Maple."

"That name is new," I reminded Jug. "Because the pageant's inclusive now, remember?" I leaned forward, letting my fingers fly across the keyboard. Miss Maple. Beauty Pageant.

I shifted impatiently, waiting to see what the microfiche database would turn up. The ancient computer whirred for what felt like ages but was probably only a few seconds. Just then, they seemed like the longest seconds of my life.

Finally, the search results popped up. Or, rather, _result_.

"One lone hit," Jughead said. "Is that even scientifically possible?"

"Apparently."

"Will wonders never cease?"

The database led us back to the microfiche archives, where we pulled out the slide we needed. I watched impatiently as Jug loaded the slide into the machine and fiddled with the focus dials. "Seriously, though," he mumbled. "Last time I checked, it _was_ the twenty-first century. If our high school has a Spacebook page, our library can scan their files to the cloud."

"And if you would like to pay for the overtime incurred in the scanning process, Forsythe, we would be happy to add that to the long list of ongoing projects," Ms. Dinkle said. Her voice was prim, but she was winking to take the edge out of her words.

"Right, of course. Budgeting—it's a mess. Librarians are underpaid and underappreciated!" he stammered, reddening.

"But not by us! We so appreciate you!" I put in. She smiled sweetly back at me.

To Jughead I said, "Are you done with your pro-technology tirade? Because"—I pointed at the screen—"there's our hit."

We leaned in, squinting. It was...

"Blank?" My heart sank. "Is there something wrong with the slide? Did we grab the wrong one?"

"Nope, I triple-checked," Jughead said. "This is the one we wanted. It just doesn't have anything we wanted on it. Ms. Dinkle," he called, leaning back in his chair to talk to her more clearly, "is there a reason there would be a blank slide in the database?"

She stood up and came over to have a look at the screen. Her long, tweedy skirt swished as she walked. It was loud in the silence of the research room—the three of us were the only ones there.

"Well," she said, frowning, "it is odd that the slide would be blank. It's a digital print of an original newspaper article."

Jughead sat up straighter, considering. "So if it's blank, that means the source material it was taken from was tampered with—"

"—and <u>that</u> means someone pulled that particular article from the paper before scanning it," I finished, cutting him off as the pieces came together in my mind. "Because they didn't want it scanned?"

Jughead nodded. "It could be." He shook his head and looked at the screen again. "But what's that smudge? Damage?"

Ms. Dinkle looked where he was pointing. "Damage? No, dear." She tilted her head. "That's not a smudge. I'm fairly certain that's the 'source material,' as you were saying. Look." She reached between us, her clothes giving off a comforting smell somewhere between mothballs and chamomile tea. She played with the dials of the machine, adjusting the resolution, until the image reformed itself into…

"That's not a smudge," Jughead said, surprised. "That's actually a photograph."

"But…of what?" No matter how I squinted my eyes, it wouldn't shift itself into something recognizable. It was like a stray puzzle piece, contextless against a void.

"Hard to say—looks like it was what was left behind, when that article was…I don't know, destroyed, I guess?" Jughead sighed. More dead ends, more banging our heads against brick walls. "Wait." Jug searched for something on his phone, then held it up to the microfiche screen to compare images.

"It's…a cross?" I said, uncertain.

"Across from what, dear? How can you tell?" Librarian Dinkle asked.

"No." I smiled. "I mean, it's a cross necklace. Like a crucifix. Don't you think?" I passed her Jug's phone, where the results of his image search revealed row after row of different crosses against different necks. She squinted at the phone, giving a half-hearted sound of agreement before excusing herself and wandering back to her desk.

The image on the microfiche was blurry and distorted, but if it looked like anything, it looked like an ornate cross dangling from a thick, sturdy chain. A small swatch of…<u>something</u> next to it might have been…

"And is that…" I reached to the screen, tracing the image with my finger. "The edge of a pocket watch?"

Jug whistled. "Good eye, Cooper. It definitely could be. A cross <u>and</u> a pocket watch."

It was our first clue. I felt a palpable hitch of excitement in my stomach. But it was quickly followed by an overwhelming sense of… overwhelm. Was this just an exercise in futility? Miles to go, I knew. A torn picture of a necklace that <u>might</u> be a cross? <u>Maybe</u> the edge of a pocket watch? Not much to go on. It was a clue, but a cryptic one. We were still basically pushing a boulder uphill.

Then again, when it came to solving mysteries, our track record was pretty solid.

"So someone ripped a photo from an old article about the Revels, and what got left behind—"

"Most likely accidentally," Jughead put in. "When will the bad guys learn: People with something to hide really ought to take the time to be thorough."

"What got left behind," I continued smoothly, "was this random section of a photo with someone wearing a cross. And maybe someone wearing or holding a pocket watch." I shook my head. "It's not much of a lead." Understatement, thy name is Betty Cooper.

"Someone religious?" Jughead asked.

"Plenty of churches nearby," I pointed out. "Maybe something about the wicked underbelly of this town makes people extra twitchy to pray?"

"I can't say it's had that effect on me, but sure," Jug said, wry. "What about the nuns? The Sisters? They might be less 'religious,' more 'bat-house crazy,' but they dress the part."

I considered it. A tiny charge of hope fluttered in my throat. But I tried to check myself. "Jughead," I said, "you know how much I would love it to be the Sisters. After everything they've done to Polly, our friends—they should be punished. They deserve so much more blame, more pain than they've gotten. But I don't want to jump to conclusions because of my feelings for the Sisters. We have to be methodical about this."

"I can be methodical," Jughead said. "I can be open-minded. But that doesn't mean we're not going to investigate the Sisters. And if they're guilty? We'll nail them to the ground."

"Sounds good," I said, "albeit gruesome. But remember, the key word is if."

We printed out the best image we could recover from the tiny scrap of a photo and thanked Ms. Dinkle for her help.

Stepping outside, I squinted against the sudden glare of the sun setting in the distance.

I blinked.

I gasped.

"What is it, Betty?" Jughead asked, his curiosity piqued.

"Everybody's favorite little cultist—four o'clock." I pointed.

Down the street, to our right, there was Evelyn again. She was huddled with Ethel Muggs, of all people, and they looked to be in intense conversation. "It's like she's following us," Jughead joked.

"I wouldn't put it past her, but I doubt that," I said. "That library was empty. We would have spotted her if she were actually spying on us. And anyway, whatever she and Ethel are talking about, it looks like they're serious about it. They haven't even noticed we're standing here in the first place."

"A mystery for another day," Jughead said, lifting my wrist to glance at my watch. "Speaking of, should we call it a night? I promised my dad I'd be home for a 'family dinner,' and if I miss it—"

"So much for pretending at 'normal,'" I finished.

He kissed me. "As always, my appetite precedes me."

A sudden gust of wind whipped through the trees, and I shivered. "A mystery for another day," indeed. The bones weren't going anywhere—and neither were we.

WEDNESDAY

CHAPTER THIRTEEN

Archie:

Still on for a lunchtime rehearsal?

Josie:

On my way. You got your guitar?

Archie:

👍 Meet you in the music room?

Josie:

Yeah, my keyboard is in the closet anyway. Might as well avoid lugging it anywhere if we don't have to.

Archie:

Got it, good call. Heading there now.

∿∿∿

Unknown Number:

Everything's ready. Will keep you posted.

∧∧∧

ARCHIE

I passed by the auditorium on my way to the music room to meet Josie, and had to take a look inside. Ronnie'd seen it earlier, and she said it was totally crazy and overrun with people doing pageant prep. I'll admit, I was curious; maybe I wasn't competing, but it was a fun enough distraction.

Inside, preparation was in full swing. *I guess we weren't the only ones who had the idea of a lunchtime rehearsal.* A bunch of kids were rehearsing for the talent portion, it looked like, and there were plenty milling around doing other pageanty things, like practicing interviews. Fangs was reading from cue cards—Jughead told me he'd given the Serpents "orders" to participate in the pageant, and Fangs had apparently had a blast walking Hot Dog in the Pet Parade—and Peaches 'N Cream kept doing that stage-mom thing of pointing at the corners of her mouth, encouraging him to smile while he read.

Meanwhile, closer to the stage, Cheryl's old-school minions, Ginger and Tina, had stuck a long strip of blue painter's tape to the floor. (I took a second to hope, for their sake, that they had permission to do that, because the new janitor is *not* kidding around.) They were wearing scary-tall high heels and taking turns walking along the blue line, waving. It looked a little crazy, but hey—I'd never been in a pageant before. Posture probably *was* important, and also things like knowing how to walk gracefully in fancy, uncomfortable shoes.

Ginger and Tina had taken a small pot of . . . Vaseline? . . . out of one of their bags, and were now making scary, bared-teeth faces while smearing the goop in their mouths. Was this a girl thing? A pageant thing? Or just a plain old weird thing? I'd have to get Veronica's take the next time I spoke to her.

Or maybe Josie would know. I checked my phone to see what time it was and realized she'd probably be in the music room by now. I went to find her, hoping she wouldn't make me ingest any kind of crude oils in the name of victory.

"Archie!"

I looked up and realized Ethel Muggs was coming into the auditorium just as I was walking out. She had a Farm T-shirt in her hands.

Since when is Ethel a Farmie? I'd have to ask Betty. Maybe I missed something.

"Hey, Ethel," I said. "Sorry, I was distracted. Didn't mean to get in your way."

"No problem," she said. "But . . . you're not in the pageant, are you? You and your dad are doing the sets, right?"

"Yeah, we're just about finished up. Everything's being stored backstage," I told her. "All that's left is a couple of booths to build for the block party."

"Cool," she said. "It should be fun."

"Yeah, definitely." I looked at the time on my phone. "I should actually get going. I'm supposed to be meeting Josie."

"Of course, Archie," Ethel said. She gave me a cryptic little smile, and walked away.

ᴧᴧᴧ

Something felt off the second I stepped into the music room. The lights were on, but it was empty, and anyone who uses this room regularly knows that we turn off the lights on our way out. It's a little pet peeve of Ms. Grundy's replacement.

The other thing that was strange was that Josie's keyboard was out and set up, though it wasn't turned on. She loved that machine. It was perfectly calibrated . . . and *very* expensive, and she treated it better than most people treat their friends. She would never have left it out like that and risk someone damaging it, or even stealing it. It was totally not her style. She was more responsible—more anal, but in a good way—than that.

The room was quiet, still. Even though the lights were on, it felt dark and eerie, and right away, my senses went on high alert. I had the feeling that someone had been in here just before me. But only music students had keys to this room . . . and while I didn't exactly do an aggressive sweep of the whole building, I hadn't seen any music students in the auditorium or in the halls on my way here, only a few stray drama kids helping some pageant contestants hem formal dresses and suits for the evening-wear portion of the show.

I took a deep breath and walked the perimeter of the room for a minute, eyes darting across every surface, even though I couldn't say what exactly I was looking for. Something, anything out of the ordinary . . . something to explain why I had the creepiest feeling that I was being watched.

That was when I heard it.

It was a low sound, quiet. Like the scratching of the mice Dad and I found nesting in our garage that one summer. I almost didn't hear it.

Then the scratching morphed into something more human. It was a banging, or a pounding. Like someone knocking their fists on a door. There was only one door in the room other than the one you come in through: the utility closet.

"Hello?" I called out, hesitant.

The pounding got louder, more insistent, and now someone was shouting, too. *Is that a girl's voice?* I thought maybe.

"Who's there?" I called. And whoever they were—*why* were they locked in a closet?

The pounding and the shouting from the closet got louder and more frantic. I could tell now, for sure, that it was a girl's voice. I scrambled to pull out my own keys and open the door.

"I'm coming," I called as I rattled the keys in the lock. "I've got it! Just step back, I'm gonna open the door."

"Archie?" The voice was high and definitely very freaked out. It was also a voice I recognized.

"Josie?" I fumbled with my keys, stabbing a few wrong ones into the lock in my hurry. The entire set landed on the floor with a loud jangle.

"Arch, what's going on out there? Tell me you've got the keys! Mine are in here with me, obviously. If you don't have a set, there's a pair in the office—"

"No, no, I have mine, just dropped them. Sorry. I've got it now." I tried again with the lock, going slower this time to be more precise. The key slid in smoothly this time. "Done." The lock gave with a satisfying *click*, and I pulled the door open, not sure what to expect.

"Archie, thank *god*," Josie said, rushing out of the closet and throwing her arms around me in a grateful hug. "I don't have a whole lot of fears, but unfortunately, claustrophobia does top off the short list." She centered herself and half closed her eyes, taking some deep breaths to calm down. "I thought I'd be in there forever."

"It wouldn't have been *forever*. We were meeting up, remember?" I thought I was being reassuring.

Josie was not reassured. Not that I blamed her. Her eyes narrowed. "Archie, it's a *phobia*. It is inherently irrational. Not to mention, when that door clicked shut behind me and I realized some . . . *some random freak* had locked me in? Yeah, my reasonable train of thought left the station. I mean, what the actual eff?"

"Seriously. You're sure someone locked you in? Like, on purpose?" It just seemed so unbelievable . . . and like she said, random. *Unbelievable* we got a lot of in Riverdale, but *random* was slightly less common.

She leveled me with a perfectly arched eyebrow. "Archie, do you think I did this for kicks and giggles?"

I shook my head, trying to backtrack. "No, of course not. Sorry, I didn't mean to imply . . . It's just that this is so *weird*."

"You're telling me. I got here earlier than I thought—I figured you'd be in here, setting up. But, you know, even if I'd known you wouldn't have been here yet, I wouldn't have, like, *worried* about being in here by myself."

"I stopped by the auditorium to see what was going on," I said, suddenly wishing I hadn't. *Would I have made it to the music room to see who had decided to lock Josie up? Would I have been able to stop it?*

"Right, I mean, normally, no big. I had plenty to do while I waited. I'm a big girl, I can take care of myself. Or so I thought."

"You can take care of yourself unless someone out there is out to get you. That's not your fault," I said, feeling terrible that I hadn't been able to prevent it. I could see Josie was not only angry, but also, underneath that and the bravado, she was seriously shaken. It was totally understandable.

"I got the lights going, took out my keyboard, and set it up. Then I went to grab my sheet music from the file cabinet. That was when I heard footsteps."

"Footsteps. Anything special about them?"

She shrugged. "No, they just sounded like regular old foot-steps. Not especially heavy or light. I was waiting on you, so the sound of it didn't exactly spark suspicion. It's a building, people walk all around it. I called out to you, even, thinking you were here. But obviously, there was no answer."

"Right. So then what happened?"

"I was just thinking I should come out of the closet and see who was there . . . when the door slammed shut. I called out—I think I said something sort of pointless like, 'Hey!' I ran to try the doorknob, but it just rattled. That was when I real-ized I was locked in."

I frowned. Super shady. But also not super big on helpful details. "Anything else?"

She sighed. "One thing. And it's *sketchy*. After I yelled out, while I was still struggling with the door? I heard laughing. Like whoever was on the other side was pretty pleased with herself."

"Herself," I said, catching the meaning behind the word. "So you think it was a girl?"

"It sounded that way," she said. She had a far-off look in her eyes like she was replaying the whole thing over again in her brain. "I don't know for sure. I mean, I can't possibly, right?"

I shook my head. I had no idea.

"You know," she said, looking helpless and stressed, "under different circumstances, I'd try to just write it off, to tell myself I was being paranoid, that it must have been a mistake. But mistakes don't ignore you when you pound on the door. And they don't *giggle*."

"No, they don't," I agreed. "I think you're right not to write this one off as a mistake."

"But, Archie," she said, her brown eyes wide, "if it wasn't a mistake . . . what was it? Who did that to me?"

I only wished I had an answer.

∿∿∿

Edgar Evernever:

Is everything on track?

Evelyn:

So I'm told by my source.

Edgar Evernever:

Wonderful. And I'm so thankful to you, dear, for your part in making sure this all runs smoothly.

Evelyn:

Of course. We're all working toward a common goal, after all. Many become one.

Edgar Evernever:

Exactly.

The first thing I hear is the laughter.

High and sweet, like the laughter of a child. Many children, in fact, all gleefully . . . reveling.

Reveling in what is to come.

When the moment of selection was upon me, in that instant I was not afraid. I'm certain that is difficult to believe. But this land is my home, and its rituals are my traditions. I can't say I fathom exactly how the selection is made, but when Mother informed me that I had been exalted, plucked from the flock, *chosen*?

In that moment, I felt a swell of pride.

Now I wait, tucked away in a small cave in the forest. Three days of solitude and reflection, to ready myself emotionally and spiritually, for the next stage of transcendence.

The final stage.

The people, they're meant to leave me be, to afford me the space and privacy to live out this time on my own terms, as I myself see fit. But the children can't help themselves. Curiosity outweighs all else, of course, and they have so many questions.

I cannot answer their questions. I daren't come out of the cave at all, save for those moments when the Elders bring me my meager sustenance.

The children grow bolder; they draw closer and chatter in ever-louder voices. The time, the day, the moment—it is nearly upon us.

I am hungry, I am tired, and yes, though it does not befit someone in my position to admit as much, I am lonely. But one thing I am *not* is afraid.

For today, we revel.

CHAPTER FOURTEEN

Reggie:

Yo—wanna bum a ride in a sick set of wheels after school?

Archie:

Sure, but can you drop me at Pop's? I'm meeting my dad there to load up some of the Cocktails and Canapes setup for Friday. We've gotta move it from Pop's to Town Hall.

Reggie:

No prob.

Archie:

What's the deal with the car?

Reggie:

Oh, you'll see.

VERONICA

After classes, Betty and Jughead were off to do more sleuthing—Betty had texted that she was headed to talk to her mom in a Hail Mary attempt to wrench any small morsel of information about the history of the Revels. So it was the perfect opportunity to squeeze in some pageant prep with Kevin. And it seemed that the entire student body agreed with us. Students were descending on the high school auditorium after classes to cram in as much Royal Maple interview prep as possible.

We grabbed some snacks from the vending machine and stepped outside for some fresh air while we waited for at least some of the pageant crush to die down.

"Remind me why we're determined to fight through the throngs?" I asked him. "You know we could totally skip out for a quick order of onion rings instead of this substandard subsistence." I waved my sad little cellophane bag at him. "The gym will still be here in thirty minutes."

"Time is money." He laughed, seeing my face. "Okay, never mind. But practice makes perfect," Kevin said, sipping a cola from a glass bottle. "And while perfection is an unrealistic standard reinforced by the deeply curated experience of being a member of our social media–driven 'influencer culture'"—he made the little air quotes as he spoke—"I'd still really like to aim for it. If we leave campus, the chance that we'll come back dwindles. They've done studies."

"Who?" I demanded.

He shrugged. "Someone, somewhere, has definitely done that study. Don't make me do research. Anyway, what can I say?" He gave me a sheepish smile. "I'm a type A with a strong need for validation. Positive reinforcement is my drug of choice."

"Well, lucky for you, my dear," I told him, "*your* manager—"

"I like to think of you as more of a mentor," he interjected.

"Whatever suits your fancy," I said. "Our priority today is getting you pitch-perfect ready with your interview responses."

"Best day ever," Kevin said, practically singing.

I laughed. Kevin's enthusiasm for . . . well, *pageantry* was kind of infectious, I had to admit.

And speaking of pageantry . . . "What is *that*?" I pointed to a sleek silver convertible cruising toward us from the student parking lot.

"It's a car," Kevin said authoritatively. "A very fancy car."

I pinched him. "That much I knew. Jerry Seinfeld's Amagansett house isn't too far from Lodgehampton; I've had better access to his car collection than half those comedians he takes for coffee."

Kevin sighed. "I just can't with you."

The car pulled up next to the school and came to a stop, two friendly faces beaming at Kevin and me. "Reggie?" I asked.

"And *Archie?*" Reggie was behind the wheel, and Archie was lounging shotgun, looking very comfortable with his ride. His hair was already endearingly mussed from the wind.

"Hey," he said. "What do you think?"

"I think . . . it's a cute car—with about a ten percent chance of being symptomatic of a midlife crisis or Napoleon complex."

"Oh, Veronica, you wound me," Reggie protested. He pushed his aviator sunglasses onto his forehead to show me his best "wounded" look.

"I'm *confident* you can take it," I said. "What the hell are you guys doing behind the wheel of this little number right now?"

"This baby? This is a vintage Datsun Z," he said, running a hand along the door lovingly.

"That explains my unfamiliarity," I said sotto voce, turning to Kevin. "My father leans heavily toward German manu-facturing."

"Well, sure," Kevin said. "As one does."

"People don't necessarily think of classic and collectibles when Mantles' Used Car Lot comes up, but we've got plenty of beauts like this in the private garage. For discerning cus-tomers only, naturally."

"Naturally," Kevin echoed, wry.

"Anyway, my pops was generous enough to loan a few of our favorites to the Motorcade. I'm helping him take them to be detailed so they'll all be ready in time. Your boy Archie just wanted a chance to ride something a little more baller than that beater jalopy of his."

"That *beater jalopy* of his is brimming with classic Americana charm," I retorted. "But if you two are having fun, Archie, by all means, enjoy."

I circled around to Archie's side of the car and leaned in for a kiss. "Call me later? This won't go late—*not* that I'm going to rush you," I quickly added in Kevin's direction, to stave off any protests.

"Definitely," Archie said. "Have you heard anything from Betty?"

I shook my head. "Anything new from Jughead?"

"Not yet."

I smiled. "Well then," I said, "I guess that means we might be free tonight."

"Good," he said. "I have—well, something weird happened earlier. I'll tell you about it later."

"Weird? Should I be worried?"

"I'm okay," he reassured me. "It didn't happen to me. And I'm not even sure if it's anything to worry about. But around here, who knows?"

"Well, now I'm intrigued. You'll have to fill me in."

"Definitely."

We kissed again. When we broke apart, Archie ran his hand through his hair, ruffling it even more. "I'll keep my fingers crossed we can meet up later."

"No crossing of fingers necessary," I told him. "We'll make it happen. Be careful," I said, squeezing his hand in a final farewell.

Although the truth was: Around here, there were plenty of reasons to keep our fingers crossed.

∿∿∿

Veronica:

B, you've been MIA all afternoon! Kev and I are at the school and it's a SCENE.

Betty:

Recon with Jug. Will fill you in later.

Veronica:

Good. Because Archie said he has something "weird" to tell me later, too.

Betty:

Weird, huh? I can't even pretend to be surprised.

Veronica:

He's okay, he swears. Will fill you in when I get the deets.

Betty:

Def. And vice versa if I hear anything on this end.

KEVIN

"Antoinette Topaz, could you please explain to the judges why *you*, above all these other, most worthy competitors, deserve to win the Royal Maple title?"

Veronica and I walked into the auditorium to find the stage littered with endless clusters of chairs set up for interviewer-interviewee role-play, and—among others (was that *Peaches 'N Cream* I saw, quizzing an unexpectedly game Fangs Fogarty?)— Toni and Cheryl happily camped out, hard at work.

Correction: *Cheryl* was happily camped. Toni looked like she might be running out of patience.

I feel you, girl, I thought. Cheryl had a lot of great qualities . . . but she was more intense than a Barneys Warehouse sample sale (as least as Veronica had described them to me). We walked over to them to say hi, but they were deep enough into their thing that they barely registered our presence. So we hovered on the periphery while Toni gathered her thoughts together, Cheryl waiting patiently with her hands folded in her lap.

"Well," Toni said, taking a deep breath and clearly working to project from her diaphragm, "in just the past year alone, I think I've shown poise and resilience. When Southside High was closed down and we students were integrated into Riverdale

High, I embraced the culture and encouraged my fellow 'Southies' to do the same. In fact, as a Southside Serpent, I've had the opportunity to hone my leadership skills and my loyalty."

"Beep!" Cheryl made a noise like a wrong-answer cue on a game show and held her arms up in a tall *X*. "Alas and alack, I must redirect this. Sorry, TeeTee, but we're going to have to take that one from the top. You're going at this one all wrong."

Toni raised an eyebrow. "Am I?"

I was slightly surprised, too—the response had seemed pretty solid, if a little less than perfectly polished. Of course, Cheryl either didn't notice or was totally undaunted by the sarcastic lilt to Toni's voice.

"Indeed, *ma chérie*," she said. "While you and I both know that the Southside Serpents have offered you the unparalleled, unconditional loyalty that not even blood kin could rival, the unfortunate fact remains that to many a straitlaced, small-minded Riverdale citizen, they are first and foremost a motor-cycle gang. Not exactly paragons of virtue and admiration."

"Cher," Toni said carefully, "are you saying you think the Serpents are . . . trashy? Or that my Serpent affiliation is something to be ashamed of?"

"Absolutely not, my beloved!" Cheryl looked utterly shocked at the mere suggestion. "I wear my Serpent jacket with unadul-terated pride. I'm only telling you what the judges might think." She bit her lip. "Please don't shoot the messenger."

Veronica nudged me. "This is . . . taking a turn."

"Agreed," I whispered back. "But the question is, should we be watching? The conversation feels not only like a slow-motion train wreck but also fairly private. It's definitely not going anywhere good."

"Um, *exactly*," Veronica said, eyes shining. "Which means that *we* are not going anywhere until it's played out. I may be a reformed mean girl, but you know I do still like a little drama. Especially when it's not mine."

"Question asked and answered. Always here for the drama, Ronnie, and I am *into* it," I said. "Honestly, I admire that about you."

The girls were still at it, of course. Toni had folded her arms across her chest, considering what Cheryl was saying. "Okay. So what do you suggest?"

"I have ideas. But I suspect you're not going to like them. They might be somewhat hard to hear, truthful though they may be."

"This is gonna be good," I breathed, clutching Veronica's arm.

"This is an inclusive pageant, TeeTee," Cheryl said. "A fact that can't be overlooked. A goddess like you is the very *embodiment* of inclusion."

Toni narrowed her gaze. "I'm sorry? Please, say more."

"You're a woman of color *and* you're bisexual! You are the essence of diversity. Wouldn't it behoove you to work that into your interview?"

Oh, Cheryl. Advocating "diversity points"? Representation is vitally important, but no one wants to feel like a cultural gesture. I knew before she even opened her mouth what Toni would have to say to that.

Toni exhaled forcefully, clearly trying to stay calm. "Cheryl, I know you mean well, and maybe you're not wrong—"

"Oh, she's definitely not *wrong*," I whispered to Veronica. "That's not the point."

Veronica nodded.

Cheryl whirled to us, eyes blazing. "Peanut gallery: If you insist on gawking, could you at least please have the decency to stay mum?"

I mimed zipping my lips in dramatic slow motion.

"Maybe you're not wrong," Toni went on, "but I'm not going to campaign to win the Royal Maple pageant on some kind of 'token minority' platform. I didn't particularly want to do this thing in the first place—*as you knew*—but you talked me into it, made me think it could be fun. *Fun.* That's all it needs to be. And exploiting my race or my sexuality feels like the opposite of casual, harmless fun to me." Her voice cracked when she repeated the word *fun* for the last time. Then she stood, her chair scraping the wooden floor. The sound made us all wince.

"Toni—" Cheryl said, tears springing to her eyes. "You know I didn't mean to insult you; it's only that I adore you, and I want you to have every possible advantage in this competition."

"*If* I have an 'advantage' just because of certain things about me that I didn't even choose, then let them *be* . . . advantageous. I don't need to straight-up exploit them."

"Well, why not, for pity's sake?"

"Because," Toni said simply, "that just feels like . . . exploiting *me*."

Ouch. I cringed, and I could see that Cheryl was reacting, as well. Her good intentions here were definitely ill-advised.

"TeeTee," Cheryl started, reaching for her, her voice shaking.

"Just—don't," Toni said, pulling back. "It's fine, I get what you were doing, what you were saying, but . . . but I need a minute."

"Toni—" Veronica said as she stalked past us.

I put a hand on her forearm. "Give her a second. It'll be okay. She just needs to have a hot minute to process."

Then I looked in the same direction Veronica had been staring in.

I don't know if Veronica had seen what I was seeing—she definitely seemed more concerned about Toni's emotional state. But there wasn't much time to think about it. My heart turned over and my pulse kicked up.

"*TONI!*" I called.

"Wait, Kevin, seriously?" Veronica asked, confused. "What about processing?"

"No!" I blurted. "Just—look!"

I pointed toward the doorway, where an enormous papier-mâché bulldog head loomed. It had been there for as long as I could remember, something some former students created in a burst of enthusiasm for one particular bygone homecoming. But now it was wobbling unsteadily, and I suddenly wondered exactly *how* long it had hung up there, and what had kept it secure all this time.

It definitely wasn't looking very secure right now.

It's going to fall, I thought, some small lizard-brain part of me registering the threat even before the rest of my body caught on to what was happening. Without any conscious thought, I propelled into motion, darting to the doorway and diving for Toni, shoving her out of the way just as the bulldog came crashing down. It shattered, kicking up a small dust storm of debris, clouding the air so my eyes teared up and the two of us began to cough.

"What the hell?" Toni asked, stunned.

"The bulldog—it was swinging around." I was shaken but trying to be calm for Toni. "I mean, I'd never seen it do that before. It just—looked like it was going to land on you." My heart was practically galloping in my chest now, thundering in my ears so loudly I was sure everyone in the room could hear it. A small crowd had gathered around, mouths agape as they pieced together what had happened.

"And it would have, surely, if not for your valiant efforts," Cheryl said, rushing over. "Thank you, truly. You've more than earned your Good Samaritan points for the day."

"Seriously, Kevin. Thanks," Toni said, looking at me gratefully.

"Are you okay?" Cheryl asked, scanning Toni for injury.

"I'm fine," Toni assured her. "Just—uh, a little weirded out. If you'd been a fraction of a second later . . ." She trailed off, looking back at me again and shaking her head.

I shuddered at the thought, but pasted on my own cheerful smile. "Well, I wasn't," I said brightly. "So let's try to focus on that."

"Hear! Hear!" Cheryl said. "Unless . . . you still need your minute?"

Toni gave a small smile. "Actually, I think now I need a different minute."

Cheryl kissed her on the forehead, leaving a perfect red set of lips in her wake. She gently rubbed it off. "You can have all the minutes you want. We can practice the rest of the interview questions at home. Or not!" she added hastily, as Toni gave her a "Really, now?" head tilt.

I watched them head out. Cheryl had had a rough go of it the last few years, and I was glad to see her in a happy, healthy relationship. Toni was good for her, there was no doubt of that.

"Well," Veronica said, "ultimately, a surprisingly happy ending for something that could have gone a whole different way."

"Yeah," I said, but I was distracted, still worried.

"What is it?" Veronica asked.

"It's just . . . that bulldog."

". . . should be bolted to the wall, if it's going to hang over a doorway that way," she said, terse and imperious.

"No—Veronica, you don't get it. Moose once told me that when he made first-string football, one of the dumb little initiation pranks he was supposed to pull for the upperclassmen was to steal that mascot."

Veronica's face immediately paled. "And I'm guessing he couldn't."

"No." I swallowed. "It wasn't bolted, but it might as well have been. I think his exact words were '*That thing isn't going anywhere unless someone a lot bigger than me wants it to.*'"

"So if the bulldog fell . . ."

"It's because someone wanted it to."

CHAPTER FIFTEEN

To: Principal Weatherbee
From: Cheryl Blossom

Principal Weatherbee,

I'll get straight to the point: I've just come from the school auditorium, where my beloved Antoinette Topaz and I were rehearsing for the Royal Maple pageant. As Toni tried to exit the room, she was nearly overtaken by the bulldog mascot that used to hang above the door.

I'll repeat myself for emphasis: *used to hang.* Which is to say, it came loose and, as of the writing of this email, sits in a pile of shards and debris in the doorway to the auditorium.

Now, while the threat of bodily harm is in itself grounds for a hefty lawsuit, you can rest assured that I won't be pursuing legal action on behalf of Antoinette. Nonetheless, I suggest you alert the custodial services to properly dispose of the mess. And might I suggest a thorough investigation to ensure that no other tragedies befall the student body under your watch.

Thank you,
Cheryl Blossom

∼∧∧∼

To: Cheryl Blossom
From: Principal Weatherbee

Cheryl—

Thank you for your concerned email. I had heard all about the fallen mascot even before you contacted me, but the additional details were certainly useful. I assure you, we are taking this incident very seriously. If we discover any indication of foul play, appropriate measures will be taken. In the meantime, I'm glad to hear that Miss Topaz is unharmed, and I urge you and all your fellow students to be vigilant until we've confirmed beyond a doubt that the accident in the auditorium was an isolated incident.

All best,
Principal Weatherbee

∼∧∧∼

To: [list—all Vixens FULL]
From: Cheryl Blossom

Dearest Vixens—

It pains me that I should have to write you with such dire and alarming news, but you should know that my beloved paramour, Toni Topaz, was the victim of a vicious and not-at-all amusing prank this afternoon. While preparing for her Royal Maple interview, Toni was nearly crushed by a falling mascot in the auditorium. Were it not for the heroic efforts of Kevin Keller, I shudder to think the injuries my darling might have sustained.

While Principal Weatherbee assures me that the administration is looking into the incident, I have my doubts. He isn't convinced that the act was one of deliberate sabotage.

I say: Watch your backs.

∿∿∿

CHERYL

"They had to wrench you from my womb with forceps."

That was my ogress mother's constant refrain. It was a gothic bedtime story of sorts at Thornhill, an elegiac meditation on the myriad ways in which I'd disappointed her simply with the burden of my existence. Simply by not being my brother Jason, the über-Blossom and heir apparent, their radiant, ruby-ringleted baby boy. We were twins, yes—but make no mistake: In our parents' eyes, we were never equal.

As if I had asked for this wretched pedigree. I knew, intrinsically, why they preferred Jason. In the secret places I dared not speak by daylight, I felt the same.

And indeed, the joke, it seemed, was on them, pouring their very beating hearts and lifeblood into grooming Jason, coddling him and melding him and coaxing him into a facsimile of themselves. Never pausing to consider that, as the very best of their essences, he might yearn for more, might actually turn his back on this blighted birthright.

Not willing to entertain that outcome, even if the alternative was as finite as death.

Ha, ha.

And now? Our operatic tumble from grace was finally complete. Jason was gone, Daddy was gone (possibly the one thing he did right, after everything went so gruesomely wrong with JJ), and the only steady beat forward was Mother's continued echo: *You are a monster. You are unlovable.*

That's what she told me. With enough conviction and enough consistency that it was hard—near impossible, really—to shut her out.

Antoinette was the first person to truly make it easier.

"You're not loveless," she said. "You're not deviant. You're sensational."

Sensational.

Small wonder I reveled in the sound of that. Still do, at every opportunity. TeeTee herself is such a marvel, I would have gobbled the words down even if they weren't a respite from years of bottomless neglect and an apathy that bordered on malevolent.

Naturally, it was hard at first, letting down my defenses. Over the years, they'd swollen to gargantuan proportions, deep moats of distance and unwavering resolve, an unflinching refusal to allow anyone past my candy-colored but no less impenetrable exterior. But for whatever glorious reason, Toni was willing to wait me out, to hold out for a time that I could accept myself, and with that, accept her love. Accept her.

Well, time has come. Now I was all in.

∧∧∧

I knew for certain that Toni had changed me—irrevocably, for the better—this summer. Whereas in the past I'd been afraid of the world beyond Riverdale, preferring instead to stay close to home, comfortably ensconced in my own tiny kingdom, when TeeTee suggested a cross-country road trip on the back of her bike, I didn't hesitate before agreeing to join her.

"Call me the Thelma to your Louise," I said, thrilled at the suggestion.

"Uh . . ." She looked at me, wary. "They *died* at the end of that movie, Cher."

I shrugged. Minor details, irrelevant to us. Nothing would dampen my spirits now that we'd put this plan in motion. "We don't have to be *exactly* like them, Tee," I said. "Just imagine wanton adventure. Gorgeous, unbridled lawlessness."

She furrowed her brow, adorably concerned. "Will you settle for semi-wanton? Let's aim for more Bikini Kill, less Rage Against the Machine. That's a level of debauchery I think we can handle."

"My dear Antoinette," I said, shaking my red mane over one shoulder, "one: There's *nothing* the two of us can't handle. And two: When it comes to musical influences, I'm one hundred percent Velma Kelly. You can be my Roxie Hart. Now"—I tossed her a black sequined knapsack—"let's pack."

⌄⌄⌄

One week later, we were tearing down I-80, surrounded by verdant green and charging toward the mountain peaks rising up in the distance, wind at our faces and hearts thudding under our Serpent leather. I rode behind Toni, arms clenched around her and inhaling the jasmine smell of her soap, the ocean salt that had seeped into her skin.

"Westward, ho!" I shouted into the vast expanse. My words were swallowed by the roar of the cars rushing by, but I couldn't contain myself.

When the iconic WELCOME TO CALIFORNIA sign came into our view, Toni pulled to the shoulder, kicking up clouds of dust as we came to a halt, both of us breathing heavily and surveying the tall swath of white lettering against the blue metal.

"Ah, the myth of the American frontier," I said. "Expansion. Domination. Exceptionalism. *Manifest destiny*. It's so . . . aggressive. So wordy. So . . ." I searched for exactly the right word to express what I was feeling.

"So dreadfully *masculine*, TeeTee." I shuddered. *No, thank you.* "Thank goodness we're here to bring some femme fatale flair to that tired old trope."

She grabbed me in a classic romance-novel clinch and kissed me like the final frame of an old Hollywood love story.

"You do give good flair, Bombshell," she said, eyes sparkling.

Our first stop was obvious: The sharp yellow arrow of the In-N-Out Burger sign beckoned to us seductively. Toni revved the engine as we idled at the drive-through. "Two double-doubles with fries," she said.

A muffled burst of static that seemed to be confirmation of our order came back—it wasn't thoroughly certain, but we chose hope—and we drove around to grab our food, settling at a picnic table out front to dig in.

"Surely it won't compare to Pop's," I said, plucking a French fry from the cardboard box, "but when in Rome . . ."

Toni wrapped her hands around her enormous burger and took an equally Herculean bite in response. Her eyes rolled up in an ecstatic expression. "I don't know, Cheryl," she said after she'd swallowed. "I mean, don't tell anyone I said so—especially not Jughead, he'd probably have my Serpent jacket for speaking heresy—but if there were anyone who could give Pop Tate a run for his money?"

She wasn't wrong. Quickly we came to understand how the franchise had garnered its prodigious reputation. The fries were perfectly crisp and salted, the burgers deliciously charred, and for a few minutes, we concentrated on our food in happy silence.

It was quick enough work. Full, I turned to Toni, brushing a pink wave back from her face. "TBH, Tee, I can't quite believe we're actually here. This road trip was just what the proverbial doctor ordered. Your best idea yet, *ma chérie*."

Toni took a long sip of her shake. "Thanks, babe. I know some Serpents who came out to LA a while back—they've been saying for ages I should come visit. Here's hoping they meant it."

I held up two crossed, crimson-lacquered fingers, the polish bold and bright in the midday sun. "Duly hoped."

I gathered up our trash and tossed it, then turned back to my literal ride-or-die. Every little glance I snuck at her made my pulse flutter. Sometimes I still couldn't believe we were together.

"So," I asked, a little mischief in my voice. "What should we do first?"

⌃⌃⌃

It was impossible to decide on one thing, so we did a little bit of everything instead.

Griffith Observatory. "I feel so *Rebel Without a Cause*," Toni said, stuffing her hands into her jacket pocket and doing her best James Dean disaffected middle-distance gaze.

I whipped out my iPhone and snapped a picture. "Funny, I was thinking *La La Land*."

"Emma Stone?" Toni shrugged. "Sure, I could see it. I get where you're going. But she's got nothing on you."

Later, as we traipsed the Hollywood Walk of Fame, we paused for a selfie on Rita Hayworth's star. "I'm a sucker for redheads," Toni admitted. "But, you know—the one in particular."

In front of the Chinese Theatre, Toni Insta-storied me crouching over Marilyn Monroe's handprints, covering them with my own. "Bombshell recognize bombshell," I trilled at the camera. And on the terrace at Chateau Marmont, we toasted and posted with a "Say, Vixen!"

By the end of the day we were beyond fatigued, contentedly

worn-out. Toni texted her Serpent contact, who was more than happy to host us at her apartment, and we headed over for a casual take-out dinner and some catching up.

∧∧∧

Warwick. The type of lounge movies about LA used to taunt the rest of us with images of how impossibly sleek and trendy their city is. It was a far cry from the Whyte Wyrm, but I guessed that LA Serpents liked the occasional dash of Hollywood glamour alongside their grit.

Delia, their clear leader and our de facto hostess, was a rail-thin spitfire with ghost-white hair and icy-gray eyes. Her LA crew was Lenny ("short for Lena but not like Lena Dunham, seriously, she'll murder you just for implying that," Delia said, when making initial introductions) and a suitably petite brunette with a *Rosemary's Baby* pixie cut named, implausibly—albeit appropriately—"Teeny" ("short for Rochelle").

Inside it was all luxe velvet seating and dim lighting, gilded chandeliers and silk pillows and cocktails that sparkled brighter, more prettily than jewels. The place was table-reservation only, but Delia "knew a guy," and that guy happened to be the manager, so lucky us. Despite the reservation policy, a line of desperate hopefuls snaked down the street past a velvet rope, which we happily stomped past.

"Step aside, plebes," I snapped, sidling up to the bouncer.

Behind me, I heard Delia snicker. Teeny mumbled to Toni, "Is this girl for real?"

"You have no idea," Toni shot back. I grinned.

"I kind of love it," Teeny said.

"You have no idea," Toni repeated. My heart swelled.

This time, I opened my mouth and cackled with sheer, unadulterated delight.

TeeTee and I wasted nary a moment racing out to the dance floor. The space was packed, the smell of pheromones and expensive cosmetics in the air. We were surrounded by models/actresses/whatevers in strappy tops and skinny jeans, but even amid all the glitz and glamour of LA, Antoinette and I stood head and shoulders above the crowd. Immediately, we gave ourselves to the music, moving with blissful abandon.

"Paradise found!" I had to shout to be heard over the steady thrum of drum and bass, but it was a fabulous excuse to brush my lips against Toni's earlobe.

She grabbed my hand in response and pulled me off the dance floor, over to the bar. Her forehead glistened, and her eyes shone. It turned out Delia knew the bartender, too—these Serpents were impressively connected, it seemed—who immediately slid two elaborate drinks our way.

We clinked and sipped. It tasted like passion fruit and bitters. Also: freedom.

I could see from her smile that Toni agreed. "Nice to be away from Riverdale, huh?" she asked.

I took a deep breath, closing my eyes and soaking it all in. "Oh, TeeTee," I gushed. "I can't tell you how freeing it is. After all those years of chasing the fantasy of my parents' approval, to be here and just . . . let it go."

"That's what I like to hear," Toni said. She stepped toward me and cupped my face in her hands. But right as her lips touched mine, she started. "Wait, what?"

When I pulled away, I saw her puzzled expression and followed her gaze.

A few seats away, at the very end of the bar, Delia and Lenny were chatting up some aggressively basic club rat lout. We sidled closer, craning to hear him.

"I mean, people say it as a joke," he was droning, "but I really am kind of a big deal."

"Oh, *obviously*," Lenny said, moving so close that he visibly tensed.

Toni made a face and mimed sticking her finger down her throat, and I nodded. Who was this unfortunate swine with the weak chin, and why were our girls wasting precious life's breath on him?

"Um . . ." Toni nudged me.

I watched. As Lenny wove a spell with her body, Delia expertly slid her fingers into his back pocket and . . . extracted his wallet? Did my eyes deceive me?

I was stunned.

"Naughty," I said to Toni. But my voice rang with admiration. Maybe *that* was why the Serpents patronized this particular, particularly high-end drinkery?

The patsy wandered off with an unsolicited promise to return with his boon companions, a dreary prospect if I'd ever heard one. Toni and I took the opportunity to ferret out the full story.

"Delia!" Toni exclaimed, giving her a playful tap. "What was that?"

"What was what?" Delia asked, playing dumb, but grinning slyly.

"Come on. We saw. You lifted that guy's wallet?"

"Damn right we did," Lenny said. "Jerk was straight-up screaming at the bartender. Like a preppy bully out of an eighties movie. James Spader is so over, girls. And we Serpents don't play that way."

"Don't get your panties in a twist," Delia said preemptively, even though we hadn't said a word. "We'll pay it forward. One of our Serpent sisters is saving for her own piercing parlor, and she could use the scratch."

Was it ethically murky? *Absolument.* I let out a tiny involuntary squeal.

Lenny turned to me, teasing. "Are you scandalized?"

"Au contraire," I said, leaning forward. The tiny hairs at the back of my neck had pricked to attention. "More like intrigued."

This, then, was what blissful abandon felt like.

Our wanton adventure had officially commenced.

᠕᠕᠕

Thirty minutes later, we were at the mezzanine bar, perched above the dance floor now and viewing the entire scene with a slight sense of remove, detachment—of an elevated vantage point, if I'm being honest, and not only because of our literal height.

"Survey says: target," I'd said, homing in on another churlish oaf close-talking an unsuspecting victim in a manner that was borderline actionable. In no time, Toni had managed to smoothly wrest him from the wounded gazelle and wrap him around her slender little finger.

"An Instagram influencer?" she said, widening her eyes in a frighteningly believable portrayal of admiration. "Tell me more."

Obviously, he was all too happy to do so. "It's all about the 'likes,'" he said, his voice nasal and self-satisfied. "You know"—he leaned in and put a hand on her elbow—"I could build your brand. My metrics are *killer*."

"'Likes' and 'metrics,'" Toni echoed. "Got it. Killer."

Meanwhile, I'd slowly crept up behind him—even if he did notice me lingering in his personal space, he wasn't about to protest his incredible so-called "luck"—and taken a page from Delia's book. His pants were tight—hipsters in LA had a rigorous and unyielding signature style—and it took me a moment to wiggle my fingers in. I grazed the edge of his wallet, and he flinched. Had I given myself away?

I thought quickly and flung myself into him, pressing my body against him as hard as I could. I used the moment to make an unabashed grab. Once I had the wallet, I shuffled back.

"Apologies, gent," I said. "Somebody pushed me, and I lost my balance."

He broke into a sleazy grin. "No harm no foul, doll."

From behind the bar, the bartender—a shaven-haired sylph with tattoo sleeves crawling up both arms—raised an eyebrow at me. I excused myself from the tête-à-tête and sidled up to the bar.

I held up the wallet and peeled a few of the larger bills from it with great flourish, fanning them out on the bar in front of her. "For your trouble, madame."

"Aren't you just a little troublemaker?" she asked, approving. "You're welcome here anytime."

I blew her a kiss as Toni grabbed me by the arm.

"Okay, Catwoman," she said, dragging me away against my protests. "You're good—why am I not surprised? But we shouldn't press our luck."

"Counterpoint . . ." said a voice from behind us.

We turned. Delia, Lenny, and Teeny were grinning like fiends, arms slung over one another's shoulders like a trio of well-coiffed musketeers.

"You don't walk away from a winning hand," Delia finished.

Without a doubt, it was a challenge.

Toni eyed me, wondering how I'd react.

I squealed again, this time with total intention. I clapped my hands together.

"This is so invigorating!"

ᗐᗐᗐ

We were stumbling across the lot, toward Teeny's car, when the rest of us saw it: a Jaguar F-TYPE in a Batmobile shade of obsidian. It had a vanity plate that read MR BIG DEAL. My gorge rose.

"I bet I know whose inferiority complex *this* little number is," I said, flashing a look at Toni. "Our very first mark of the evening."

"Hmm," Lenny said, peering into the window. "Want to make him our last, too?"

"Ooh," gasped Teeny, looking into the window on the passenger side herself now. "Do I spy with my little eye a Birkin bag? That jerkwad has a girlfriend?"

"A girlfriend with expensive taste," Lenny said.

"That's just all kinds of wrong," Toni said, looking mournful.

"Love never does play fair. But we can do our part to even the score." I took a turn ogling the bag. Whoever she was, she had good taste, even if it was high-end. Not in companions, mind you—her beau was strictly low-rent, all the way—but her aesthetic eye was killer. "Limited edition. Ostrich skin in cobalt.

Covetable." Mumsie had two—in varying shades of Blossom red, of course.

"That bag would pay our rent for a year," Teeny said, bitterness tinged with a touch of longing.

A tingling feeling crept up my spine then, sparking an electric buzz that flooded my skin. I felt impulsive, dangerous. *Even the score*, I thought, feeling wild.

Feeling *powerful*.

"In that case, it's a done deal. If you like it," I said, "let's go get it."

I began to scramble along the curb looking for a sizable rock: *All the better to smash your windows with, my pretty.* "Find me something heavy, allies!"

"Okay, I *totally* love this girl," Teeny mused, chuckling.

"Oh, girl. You have *no* idea . . ." Toni replied. It had become a sort of catchphrase for the evening. Her voice was far-off, floating to me from another world.

I felt her fingers close around my wrist. She pulled me up to my feet and away from the curb. "Which is why I won't let you be the next Riverdale vigilante to be locked away."

She leaned in, so close her lips almost brushed my own. "Cher, you are *totally* lovable . . . and totally impossible. Don't do this."

I yelped, stunned to be pulled so abruptly out of the moment. I looked down at my palm, wrapped as it was around a sizable rock. All at once, the adrenaline rushed from my veins.

Was I . . . had I just been about to . . . break into a car?

The high of my loosely Robin Hood–esque merriment vanished as quickly as it had come on, leaving me humiliated. What had I become? Wanton adventure was one thing. This was serious crime.

I wasn't Thelma or Louise—I didn't want to be. As Toni pointed out, they die at the end of their movie. Whereas I have so much to live for. In particular, Toni herself.

"I'm a fool," I groaned. "And no better than the cesspool of moral turpitude from whence I came." My eyes welled.

Toni draped her arm over my shoulder, running her fingers through my hair. "Wrong again, girl," she whispered. "Not better. *The best.* And you *don't* have to prove you're a badass to me. I kinda had you pegged from moment one. Why do you think I was crushing so hard?"

I turned to her, eyes still wet and teary, and heart filled with gratitude. I couldn't remember when in my life I'd felt so appreciated, so seen. "Antoinette Topaz . . ." I said, my voice trembling, "what would I do without you?"

She rested her arms on my shoulders, clasping her palms behind my head, at the nape of my neck. She traced circles in my skin with her fingers. "How about," she said, leaning in for a kiss, "let's not find out?"

Instead of answering, I gave myself over to the kiss. I knew she understood just exactly what my heart was trying to say.

Toni was the first person—other than JJ, of course, but that was different—who truly saw me. Saw me, and loved me for myself.

Today's accident reminded me of one thing: If *anyone* out there tried to harm so much as a candyfloss hair on her head, they'd have to answer to *moi*.

CHAPTER SIXTEEN

JUGHEAD

"So what next?" I stood on the steps of the school, shivering a little in my Serpents jacket. It felt like overnight the weather had gone from autumnal to borderline frigid.

"I . . . guess we have to find *some* way of cross-referencing the torn article from the library," Betty said, looking helpless. "But I don't know what way that is, Juggie. I mean, I don't know how many other online searches there are, or where else I could even find information about old newsp—" She stopped as it hit her. A smile spread over her face. "No, wait. Actually, I *do* know where I could find information about the newspaper."

I nodded, getting it. "Because you have a connection in the industry. Your mother, formerly of the *Riverdale Register*." I looked at her. I couldn't believe it had taken us this long. "Why didn't we think of this sooner?"

"Because my mother is insane, and the chances of her actually being helpful are basically below zero," she said, not missing a beat. "Also: We've been pretty busy."

"Well," I protested. "If chances of getting anything from her are zero, so be it. If we come out empty-handed, we're in the same place we started, aren't we?"

"Yes," Betty said darkly, "we would be the exact same amount of screwed we are right now."

"Oh, sweetie," I teased. "Your positivity is simply an inspiration."

I got her to laugh, at least. But her laugh was hollow.

∧∧∧

We headed straight to the Cooper house on my bike. When we got there, though, we realized there was a car in the driveway that we didn't recognize.

"Any idea who's in there?" I asked.

She shook her head. "Which just means it's even odds it's someone I don't especially want to see."

Someone from the Farm, she means. "Want to take a minute to get, like, ready for this?" I asked, sensitive to how she must be feeling.

"What?" She turned and looked at me, first as though she hadn't even realized I was standing there, and then, as what I said sunk in, like I was absolutely out of my mind. "No, Juggie, I'm fine to go inside. I'm mad as hell at my mom and Polly, and you can bet just being in the vicinity of any Farmies gets me crazy upset all over again—but I'm fine. I promise. But before we go in there, you have to see *this*."

She held up her phone so the screen was just inches from my face.

Kevin:

911, Nancy Drew. Incident at the pageant. Falling mascot on Toni.

Betty:

The mascot from the auditorium? Is she hurt?

Kevin:

Yes, and no, but she could've been. And it's looking like that's what someone wanted.

Betty:

So she was targeted?

Kevin:

IDK if Toni herself was being targeted, but someone definitely tampered with that mascot. I watched that thing topple. I shoved her out of the way myself.

Betty:

Good job, Kev! But also, be careful!! It could have been you.

Betty:

Wait—Veronica said something weird happened with Archie and Josie. Similar?

Kevin:

Maybe? I only have rough details—Josie got stuck in a closet in the music room? She thinks she was locked in?

Betty:

So, maybe related. And maybe connected to the body in the time capsule. Crap.

Kevin:

Not the most implausible theory.

Betty:

Okay. Well, like I said, BE CAREFUL. And keep an eye and ear out for any clues. I'm at home, about to try to pump Alice for information on the time capsule.

Kevin:

Oh, Betts . . .

Betty:

I know. Operative word: TRY. But we think we have a small lead, and she may be the only one who can help us find the thread. God help us.

In that case, I wish you Godspeed, Betty Cooper.

When I finished reading, I looked up to see Betty staring at me, impatient for me to be done so we could both be all caught up.

"Well?" Her eyes were wide with meaning. "Someone is messing with stuff at school while people are preparing for the pageant, aka a Revels event. Josie supposedly got locked in a closet. And then Kevin saved Toni from a falling mascot in the auditorium."

"Okay. That feels . . . borderline pattern-ish."

"Yeah." Her eyes were wide. "And meanwhile, the time capsule that kicked the Revels off in the first place contained human bones." She gave me a meaningful "Connect the dots, Jug" look.

"I mean . . ." I sighed, considering. "The connection to a body in a barrel and accidents happening around school is . . . slightly tenuous? For all we know, that bulldog mascot was loosened well before this happened, and someone's plot just took a lot longer than they planned to go into effect."

"Something happening to Josie and then something happening to Toni? Less tenuous. And even if the connection to the Revels is less obvious, I don't know . . . Two super-shady things that both began around the same time . . ." Betty arched an eyebrow at me. "The accidents are connected to the pageant. And the pageant and time capsule are both connected to the Revels. That's more than enough of a link."

"True. And how often is a coincidence just a coincidence in Riverdale, anyway?"

"Which means that we have to at least *entertain* the possibility that they're two shady sides of one much larger, totally shadier coin."

"Also true," I said, taking her hand. "I'm right there with you. This is me, entertaining it."

Betty set her jaw, a determined glint coming into her eye. "If my mother knows *anything* at all about this, you can bet I'm going to get it out of her, one way or another."

"Oh, I'd never bet against you, Betty Cooper. That would be a fool's game."

I gave her hand a reassuring squeeze, and we went inside.

∧∧∧

Of course, it was just our luck that Evelyn Evernever was the first person we saw when we walked inside. Betty certainly hadn't been wrong about who her mother's guests would turn out to be.

Evelyn was in the living room, seated on the floor in front of the coffee table, wrapping up . . . what looked like gift bags? In front of her lay a giant tangle of gauzy white drawstring bags, a huge tin of what looked like some kind of small chocolate candies, and spools of ribbon in big, lazy coils.

"What was I saying about even odds?" she whispered to me now.

"Betty! Jughead!" Evelyn looked up and waved enthusiastically. "Betty, your mother had no idea Jughead would be stopping by."

I inhaled sharply, seeing Betty clench her fists hard enough to break glass through the corner of my eye.

"Yes," Betty said, offering a small grin, "it was kind of a last-minute thing. Sorry to barge in. Is it a bad time?" Her voice dripped with sarcasm. "I had no idea you'd be here. In my house. Hanging out."

"Of course it's not a bad time!" Evelyn said. "This is your home, Betty. No matter where you stand with your mother and your sister regarding your trust issues."

I reached out one arm so it stretched across Betty's torso. *Easy.* Evelyn was trying to get her riled up; it wouldn't do to let it happen.

Betty took a deep breath and managed a tight smile. "That it is, Evelyn. That it . . . definitely is. And"—she glanced at the heap of glittery supplies on the table—"it looks like *you're* really making yourself at home here, too."

Evelyn gave a little laugh. "Your mother insisted. She's such a sweetheart. It's been wonderful. I've just been assembling the gift bags for Friday's Cocktails and Canapés," she gushed.

"Your mother is outside in her cutting garden, gathering some perennials for a few of the centerpieces." She shrugged. "Mayor Lodge gave her a budget to order flowers, but you know your mom—she wanted to add a personal touch. Make it really special."

Another strained smile. "How neat. And speaking of my sweet mother," Betty went on, "I think I'm going to step outside and have a quick talk with her. If you don't mind."

"Oh, Betty." Evelyn gave a light laugh again, this time sounding more forced. "You're such a hoot. Of course I don't *mind*. I'll just be in here, if she needs me."

Betty clenched her jaw. "I'll be sure to let her know."

∧∧∧

"What exactly are you asking me, Betty?"

Alice's voice was growing flat. We were in the cutting garden now, a small enclosed patch behind the patio where the barbeque grill lived. Betty and her mother side by side on a small stone bench. A large pair of dented pruning shears that had seen way better days lay beside Alice. Sitting there on the bench, teeth opened into a slight yawn, tilted toward Betty, the tool managed to look more than a little bit ominous.

"Mom," Betty said, patience rapidly draining from her tone. This was the third time she'd tried to get an answer from her mother about news archives, and the replies were getting less and less promising—and less and less polite. "I'm *telling* you: Juggie and I went to the library to try to find more information about the history of the Riverdale Revels. We wanted to have . . . historical context for our *Blue and Gold* article. And there was nothing there. *Nothing*."

"And?" She tilted her head as if saying, *What do you want* me *to do about it?*

"*And?* Don't you think that's strange?" I put in. "This is apparently a huge deal of an event that everyone celebrated for more than a century and then *poof.* Gone. It's done, no one does it anymore, and there's not a single written record of it anywhere in our local papers?"

"No, that's not *quite* true, Jug," Betty interjected. "There actually *was* one single written record." Alice's eyes widened. "Yes, it's true, Mom—we found exactly one news article about the original Miss Maple pageant. Or, we thought we did. Because when we went into the microfiche archives to dig up the article, it wasn't there. Someone had tampered with the slide."

"Well, then, I guess you're at a dead end, Elizabeth," Alice said, terse. "Which I can only hope means you'll be leaving me to my Farm responsibilities?" She rolled her eyes. "Or is that too much to ask?"

Betty's eyes welled up. "Mom, why are you being this way?"

she demanded. "This is the sort of weird cover-up thing you normally *live* for. Why would you not want to get to the bottom of this?" She glared. "What are you *hiding*?"

Alice gave a huff and crossed her arms over her chest. "For the millionth time, Betty, *I'm not hiding anything.* I am *busy with the Farm.* I don't know why you're so determined to paint me as some great conspirer." Her voice softened. "I get it: You don't like the Farm."

"I don't *trust* the Farm."

"Yes, you've made that perfectly clear," Alice said. "And while I don't like *that*, I suppose, for now at least, I do have to accept it."

"I . . . I'm sorry, Mom." Betty did sound truly sorry—and Alice did seem truly hurt. Emotions were running high out here.

"Don't be sorry, Betty, be *smart*," Alice said. "If the mayor says it was a prank, and the one article that might be helpful has been damaged, then you're at a dead end." She wagged a gloved finger at us. "If there's one thing the two of you should have learned by now, it's that digging around for trouble in this town will only lead to you finding some. Is that really what you want?"

I stepped closer. "Not a *complete* dead end," I clarified. "Because whoever tried to disappear that article left a fragment of a photo behind. And eventually, we'll be able to trace that photo to its document of origin."

Alice stood, her face flushed and her eyes shining. Her distress was visibly rising. "Now, see here, you two—" she started.

"It's a *body*, Mom," Betty said, incredulous, cutting her off. "I hate to break it to you, but the trouble is *here*."

"It's a *joke*," Alice said, her voice thin. "It's some subhuman's sick idea of a joke! So let sleeping fake bones lie!"

"Too late for that," I said. "Seeing as how we dug it out of the time capsule and all. Cat's out of the bag. Or the barrel, as it were."

"*Jughead Jones*." Alice shot me one of her patented classic withering looks. She always managed to make my name sound like the lowest of insults in her mouth. It was the abject lack of respect, I think. "You think you're so clever. Shaking trees to dredge up silly ancient history that couldn't possibly be any use in the here and now."

"Mom—" Betty reached out, trying to calm her. I swallowed. Maybe we'd pushed too far. Alice was strong willed and outspoken, but she was also vulnerable, fragile in a lot of ways. It was how she'd managed to get swept up in the Farm in the first place.

"I think you've done enough, Betty." The voice that echoed from behind us was firm and we turned to it instantly. Polly Cooper was staring us down with what could only be described as full-on malice in her eyes.

"Polly," Betty tried, "we just wanted—"

"I don't care what you *wanted*," she spat. "Whatever you *wanted* means that Mom is a wreck. I don't know what kind of little games you and your Detective Holmes boyfriend are playing, but you have no right to come traipsing over, into our calm, peaceful *home*, and start asking questions that clearly upset people." Her voice was shaky, verging on hysterical.

"It's okay, Polly," Alice said. She had pulled herself together a little bit. "I'm fine. It's just that Betty and Jughead's questions were interfering with my personal psychic frequency." She glared at us. "Your energy is really quite toxic, did you two know that?"

"Yes, *my* energy," Betty said dryly. "Definitely."

"We're sorry for . . . *frequenting* on you," I said, barely able to fathom the words coming out of our mouths.

Alice straightened and dusted some lingering soil off the front of her jeans. "Apology accepted," she said, snappish. She fixed her gaze on Betty. "Elizabeth, I only hope that the next time you take it upon yourself to embark on an impromptu visit, it's for more pure-hearted reasons. All this stress and sub-terfuge can't be good for your digestion."

Betty shot her mom an "Are you kidding me?" look as Alice flounced off. Then we were alone, face-to-face with the wrath of Polly.

Polly stepped closer to Betty, so their noses were almost

touching. It was a sister face-off, and from the looks of it, both were eager to come out of this the dominant one.

Too bad there could only *be* one.

"Mom may accept your apology," Polly said, "but I don't. Not yet. If you truly want us back in your life in an authentic way—"

"I do, Pol, of course I do. You know that," Betty said. "But it can't happen as long as you two are brainwashed by this low-rent Manson-family knockoff. I mean, come on!"

"Funny," Polly said, but she didn't sound like she found it amusing at all, "because *I* was going to say exactly the opposite. From where I sit? It can't happen until *you* come to embrace and accept the Farm. Even if you'll never be a Farm sister yourself, you need to be okay with the fact that Mom and I *are*."

"I know," Betty said sadly. She seemed to come to some sort of realization, her features softening slightly. She stood on tiptoes to give Polly a gentle kiss on the cheek.

"What are you doing?" Polly stammered, pulling back.

"See ya, Polly," Betty said quietly.

Polly looked upset but no less determined. She squared her shoulders, then leaned to pick up the pruning shears Alice had left behind. As she moved, I saw a glint of silver at her collarbone. My pulse stuttered and kicked into overdrive.

"Polly," I said, trying to sound calm, curious, "where did you get that necklace? It's so original."

"This?" She rubbed it between her fingers, musing. "It was a gift from Nana Rose. Back when Jason and I first told her we were getting married. I tried to refuse, seeing as how she'd already given us her ring. But she insisted. Said I could think of it as an engagement present." She looked wistful for a moment. "Such a sweet woman. I never get to see her anymore."

"Truly," I agreed. "She's always been very kind to Betty and me when we've seen her. And she has really unique taste. I don't think I've ever seen a cross like it before. All that filigree."

But I had, though. Seen it before. That was the thing.

Seeing Polly's necklace dangling, I realized—

Our "photo" was blurry and hard to make out, but I'd be . . .

Well, I'd be the Farm's new convert if that cross wasn't exactly the same one we saw in the torn Miss Maple article.

∧∧∧

Edgar Evernever:

You're all finished with the gift bags?

Evelyn:

All packed up and ready for Friday night. They're waiting in Sister Alice's garage.

Edgar Evernever:

Excellent. The one becomes many and the many become one. Such is the profound and transformative power of working toward a common goal.

Evelyn:

Absolutely. I am always happy to do what's best for the Farm.

CHAPTER SEVENTEEN

Cheryl:

Dear cousin, there was another incident. Or perhaps you've already heard from Archie?

Betty:

I only got broad strokes about both incidents from Kevin. Josie in a closet and then Toni having a near miss with that mascot in the auditorium?

Cheryl:

Exactly. Your strokes are less broad than you might think. Toni's brush with bodily harm happened earlier today. We might have assumed it was an isolated event—a nearly tragic accident—but after hearing about Josie's experience, we've reconsidered.

Cheryl:

Both would-be victims are fine, thank goodness. But I think you'll agree, we can no longer pretend that nothing is amiss. TWO random incidents?

Betty:

Don't seem very random side by side. I agree.

Will you meet us at Thistlehouse for a calming mug of chamomile? TeeTee and I are here with Josie, we can fill you in.

Betty:

We'll call V and Archie and be there ASAP.

∿∿∿

BETTY

Dear Diary:

The plot thickens.

When we got to Thistlehouse, we found Cheryl, Josie, and Toni huddled in front of a fire, a cozy-looking blanket draped over Josie's shoulders. Archie and Veronica were there, too, having beaten us to the house. (Kevin was apparently riding his adrenaline rush from his heroics earlier in the day to cram in some extra pageant prep—but far away from the school, at Josie and V's insistence.) A tea tray had been set out on the coffee table with a pretty array of cookies, and Jughead wasted no time in scooping a few up in one swift grab.

Apparently, Cheryl truly couldn't stop herself from offering a slight barb. "Funny," she said, raising an eyebrow at Jug. "In times of extreme stress, so many of us actually <u>lose</u> our appetites."

Jughead wasn't remotely fazed. "Yeah, I heard something about that once." He wagged his own eyebrows at her. "Wild."

I shook my head, waving all the banter away. I took a seat in an overstuffed chair catty-corner to Toni and Josie, who was staring off into the fire vacantly. "First of all: Are you guys okay?"

Toni shrugged and nodded simultaneously, and I saw Cheryl give her hand a tight squeeze. Meanwhile, Josie turned to look at me. The flames from the fire made shadows dance over her cheekbones as she spoke. "I mean, physically, I'm fine. I was locked in, but I wasn't hurt, not like Toni. It was just creepy as hell."

"Well, yeah. And you think it was a girl who did it?" Jughead put in.

She shrugged. "I heard a girl's voice, laughing. Does that mean it was a girl for sure? I don't know. But who else would that have been?" She shuddered and pulled the blanket tighter around her shoulders.

"I just..." Archie looked pained, revisiting the memory. "I didn't see anyone or anything out of the ordinary. I...obviously wasn't paying attention."

"Archiekins," Veronica jumped in, "how could you have been? Not knowing anything was amiss, what would you have been on the lookout for?"

"Undoubtedly the same feeble-minded scoundrel who nearly maimed my TeeTee for life with that befouled bulldog mascot," Cheryl spat.

"'Undoubtedly' may be a stretch," Jughead said, "but yeah, Betty and I are basically on the same page: Two random acts of sabotage can't be random...or unconnected. It's Occam's razor: The most obvious answer is usually the correct one."

"So the question is," I said, "why? Why you two? Can you think of any reason why someone—a girl, maybe, based on the laughter—would have it in for either of you guys?"

"For both of you guys," Jughead corrected. Both girls shrugged. Josie shifted in her seat, looking slightly uncomfortable for a moment, but she didn't say anything.

"But also—what if the attacks weren't targeted?" I said, considering it. "I mean, it could be that someone is trying to sabotage the Revels, and maybe Toni and Josie were just in the wrong place at the wrong time. Well, places, plural." I looked at them again. "Can you think of anyone who might have been wandering around, right before or after your...well, let's call them accidents?"

They both shook their heads emphatically. "It was the auditorium, and people were practicing their pageant interviews," Toni said. "I mean, everyone was there."

"Okay, well, that narrows it down," Jughead quipped.

Cheryl glared at him. "Excuse me, vagrant Philip Marlowe, but if you aren't taking my girlfriend's would-be assault seriously, I will show you the door."

"We're taking it seriously," I assured her. "I still think it's worth working under the assumption that the Royal Maple sabotage and the body in the Revels time capsule are connected."

"Well, then—work under it!" Cheryl said, frustrated. "By all means. What are you waiting for, Nick and Nora?"

I glanced at Jug. He didn't have any better answer than I did. What were we waiting for? It was easy—and dispiriting.

We were waiting for another clue.

But it didn't look like any more clues would be forthcoming, anytime soon.

THURSDAY

CHAPTER EIGHTEEN

Hey, V—you around? I would love to run a few theories by you. Maybe grab Archie, too?

Veronica:

I'm just heading to school to do a trial run with Kevin on his makeup for the pageant, can you meet in an hour?

Betty:

No problem. Ttyl

⌒⌒⌒

VERONICA

I glanced around the small backstage dressing rooms that had been cleared up to give students space to prepare for the pageant. It was a similar setup to what we'd had for *Carrie: The Musical,* which was amateur but doable—barely—but it cast a certain pall over the proceedings. If memory served, *Carrie* was the last time Riverdale had gone all-out to put on a show (excluding those featured at my speakeasy, of course), and it had ended in unthinkable tragedy.

At the rate we were going, the pageant—and indeed, the entire Revels—felt destined to head in the same direction. I hope whatever theories Betty and Jughead had in mind panned out.

"Well, this dressing room feels a little less 'Miss Galaxy,' and a little more *Toddlers and Tiaras*, if you ask me. But I suppose that in the words of everybody's preferred wise old sartorial uncle, Tim Gunn, we can make it work."

"Yes, yes," Kevin said, grinning, "we know you're such the urban sophisticate, Veronica. But this will be just fine for our purposes. Now come sit." He patted the swivel chair next to his own, both situated just in front of an enormous lighted vanity mirror. The vanity table was practically buried, strewn with enough stage makeup to paint the entire cast of *Wicked* every day, twice a day, for its entire Broadway run.

"I must say, I'm excited to put on my face. Now, keep in mind: It should be dramatic enough to be seen by the judges in the front row of the auditorium, but still, and I quote, 'soft and natural.' That's what all the ViewTube videos say."

"Videos. You're so cute," I teased. "Fear not, sweet Kevin," I assured him. "Need I remind you, you're looking at a young woman who keeps Gwyneth's own personal makeup artist on retainer for special events? Veronica Lodge knows all the tricks of the trade." I arched an eyebrow. "My promise to you: This girl can contour circles around Kim Kardashian."

Kevin swiveled his chair to me, jutting his chin out to offer me his face as a canvas. "Sculpt me as you will, my master."

"With pleasure," I said, flicking the vanity lights up to their brightest setting and grabbing a marbled silicone sponge. I squeezed out some foundation in one shade darker than Kevin's natural skin tone and began to dab. The motion was soothing.

"It's like connect the dots, but on your face," I told him, smiling as I went about meticulously blending. "And can we talk about your bone structure? You're my own life-sized Ken doll."

"Flattery will get you everywhere. I'm pretty easy that way."

"Well, I assure you, there's plenty more where that came from. Stay tuned."

Once the foundation was thoroughly blended into his skin, I picked up an oversized powder brush. I dipped it in a pot of loose setting powder and began to sweep the brush over his face.

"These cheekbones, Kevin," I said. "It's a wonder you haven't been murdered by a jealous competitor yet." It killed me that kindhearted Kevin hadn't yet found his OTP. In addition to being straight amazing, my boy was a stone fox. They say God doesn't give with both hands, but Kevin Keller was the exception that proves the rule.

"Well, now you jinxed us," he said, rolling his eyes. "Especially when you consider that there have already been two random close calls around here. And trouble always comes in threes."

"Yes, yes," I muttered. "I know Betty's theory about the Revels. And there is a certain, unsettling logic to it. Not to mention, my girl's hunches are usually right. But I think we're safe, for now. Bear in mind, this is a beauty pageant, not 'the Scottish play,' and I don't think there really is such a thing as a cursed production."

"Not *cursed*," Kevin started, "more li—" He stopped, abruptly, beginning to cough.

"Are you okay?" I asked, when it seemed like the coughing fit was intensifying rather than dying down. His eyes began to tear. "Let me get you some water." I rose to do that, and he reached out to me.

"What is it?" I asked, starting to panic.

Kevin couldn't respond, though, beyond shaking his head. His cheeks were turning a terrifying shade of red, and his eyes were going glassy. "Can't . . . breathe . . ." he managed to wheeze.

"Oh my god, Kevin!" I jumped up and grabbed my phone, dialing 911 and sending out a silent prayer that I wasn't too late.

"Hold on," I begged him as the phone rang in my hand. "Just hold on, okay?"

His eyes told me he was trying to; he was truly trying. But just then, I felt anything but confident that this would all be okay.

PART THREE: REPARATIONS

CHAPTER NINETEEN

Veronica:

B, come ASAP. It's Kevin.

Betty:

What's going on?

Veronica:

SEVERE allergic reaction to his stage makeup. Anaphylactic shock. We're at the hospital now.

Betty:

Oh my god! Is he OK?

Veronica:

He will be now. Not sure what he was reacting to, though. Kev didn't even know he had any allergies.

Betty:

Thank god he's stable. We're on our way. Don't worry, we'll figure it out.

～～～

Archiekins, can you come to the hospital? It's Kevin.

Archie:

Of course—Betty just texted me. I'll be right there.

∧∧∧

VERONICA

Archie, Betty, and Jughead must have chased the speed limit mercilessly, because they seemed to burst through the door to Kevin's hospital room only seconds after I sent my last text. "Kevin!" Betty exclaimed the minute she set eyes on him. "Oh, god, you look—"

"I know," Kevin said ruefully. "My face is puffier than Kylie Jenner's lips. It's a . . . look?" He smiled at us through grotesquely swollen features: His own lips were indeed a formidable match for the youngest Kardashian's, and his eyes were nearly swollen shut. His neck was covered in red splotches. "There's no way I'm going to be in any shape to participate in the pageant by Saturday."

"Please, no more of that," I shushed him. "It's only Thursday, so who knows. But the pageant should be the last thing on your mind right now. I'm just relieved you're okay. It looked really touch and go there, for a minute." Tears rose in my eyes. I tried to keep them at bay, not wanting Kevin or the others to see exactly how worried I'd been, how doubtful that it would all end without serious, permanent bodily harm. "The way you went from *okay* to *anaphylaxis* . . ." My voice cracked. So much for stoicism.

"And you've never had any allergic reactions before?" Archie asked.

"Hives, once in a while, from a weird laundry detergent. Nothing like this, nothing life-threatening. The doctor said if the EMTs had been five minutes later in getting to me . . ." He trailed off, and I shuddered.

"Did either of you see anyone lurking around backstage around the time you had your allergy attack?" Jughead asked, pacing back and forth intently in front of Kevin's bed.

I looked at Jughead. "No, definitely not. And I was on high alert after everything that happened yesterday."

"Okay," Kevin said slowly. "But, like, how would anyone have even known that I'd have an allergic reaction to . . . something? I've never had a serious allergic reaction to anything at all, in my life."

"They didn't know anything about it. The person who tampered with your makeup had no idea this would happen."

We all turned in unison to look toward the doorway. And all our jaws dropped as we realized who was standing there.

"Ethel?" Betty asked. "Um, hi." We all liked Ethel Muggs . . . but we were surprised to see her just then.

"Ethel!" Archie sounded more than surprised now. He sounded like he was having a full-on eureka moment. "You were walking down the hallway at school when I went to meet Josie in the music room."

"And didn't Josie say she heard a girl's voice laughing outside the closet door?" I asked, putting it together. My stomach clenched as the pieces fell into place.

Archie's face flushed in fury as he processed this. "She did. And—I *saw* you! We talked! I waved; you waved back." Somehow, this detail seemed the most egregious to Archie. "Right before I found Josie locked in that closet. And you pretended everything was . . . fine and dandy—normal!"

"In her defense, there's no such thing as 'normal' in this town, anyway," Jughead quipped, then hastily sat down in a chair, abashed, when he realized no one was exactly in the mood for his sardonic bon mots.

"I know," Ethel said quietly. She looked abashed, more subdued than I was accustomed to seeing her. "I'm sorry." With a loud heave, she burst into noisy, ugly sobs. They seemed genuine, and Betty and I rushed to pat her back and settle her in a chair beside Kevin's bed.

Betty shot Jughead a quick look. "Can you get Ethel some water, please?

He held up his hands, mea culpa. "Sure, no problem. On it."

As he walked out of the room we heard a small collision, person on person, from the sound of it. It was followed by an indignant shriek. "Pardon *you*, street urchin!"

As Jughead continued in search of a vending machine, Cheryl burst into the room, Josie and Toni right behind her. Toni made a questioning face at the sobbing Ethel at Kevin's bedside, and I mouthed a quick "We'll explain later."

Josie carried a bouquet of stick balloons that she set down on Kevin's tray table as she kissed him hello. "How are you feeling, hun?" she asked. She winced, looking him over. "I'm assuming not awesome."

"You assume correctly. Thanks for those, Josie," Kevin said. "I'm looking forward to getting a better look at them when the swelling goes down. And to answer your question, I'm feeling better, now that they've got me on an IV."

He propped himself up and tried to fix his gaze—the little of it he had—on me. "Veronica, I love you, but did you call the whole junior class?"

"Sorry," I said. "I wasn't thinking we'd all be in this room at the same time, when I sent out all the texts. I guess it's a bit much. But I knew Josie would want to know. I mean, that much was a given, yes?"

"I'm your sister now, guy," she reminded him, "not to mention I was a target, too."

"And since TeeTee *also* had a brush with the grim reaper," Cheryl put in, "we all thought a sit-down was in order. However, it seems that this mystery may have already been solved." Cheryl shot a withering gaze at the inconsolable Ethel, having clearly put two and two together.

Toni gave him a smile. "Also, we wanted to see how you were doing, Kevin. Glad you're okay." She whirled to face Ethel. "No thanks to you, though, I'm guessing?" She crossed her arms in a vaguely threatening manner.

Ethel didn't protest. "I am *so sorry*—to all of you. It was an awful plan. But—it wasn't mine."

"Really?" Jughead asked dryly, reentering the room with a bottle of water. "Because to the naked eye, it really looks like it *was* your plan. What with how you came in here and said *you did it* and everything."

"No—I did, but it was—"

"Evelyn!" Betty interjected, her eyes lighting up.

Ethel nodded, miserable. "Yeah. Evelyn put me up to it. She wanted to sabotage the pageant."

"Evelyn *Evernever*? Why?" Jughead asked.

"We *saw* the two of them conspiring the other day, when Jug and I were coming from the library!" Betty cried, equal parts shocked and livid. She looked at Jug. "Remember?"

"I do," he said. He made a face. "I can't believe it took me this long. We should have put it together sooner."

"We were doing it—the sabotage stuff—together," Ethel continued. "Well, I locked Josie in the music room"—Josie shot her a miffed look—"and Evelyn did the makeup swap."

"She was carrying all that makeup stuff the other night, at the after-party!" Archie said. "Man, I *knew* that seemed strange! But I didn't say anything because, I mean—whatever, she had a bag of lip glosses, it didn't exactly seem like a federal crime." Archie frowned. "Speaking of *should have put it together sooner.*"

"No, Arch—none of us got it," Betty said, moving to him and rubbing his forearm reassuringly.

"Yeah," Ethel said, jumping in. "Evelyn had bought some stuff, different products, to see how she could tamper with them. We played around with different ideas, that night after the La Bonne Nuit party. Then she left them in the dressing rooms. She didn't know it would be Kevin who used them! She just swapped out some of the makeup that had been stored in one of the dressing areas for her own stuff."

"I didn't recognize the brand," Kevin said. "I thought you'd bought it, Ronnie."

"I thought it was *yours*," I said, feeling a pang of guilt for not being immediately more suspicious. *One more passenger aboard the "should have known" train.*

"And the bulldog that almost annihilated Toni?" Cheryl snapped.

"That we had to rig together." Ethel looked miserable and totally abashed.

"Teamwork. Beautiful," Jughead quipped. "Must be some of those down-home Farmie values."

She flinched at his words. "Well, that's just it. She said the pageant went against everything the Farm stands for—modesty, unity, equality. Her father *insisted* that she participate—and get all the other kids to participate, too. She was furious, but she felt trapped."

"So she sabotaged the pageant, putting everyone in danger, instead," Betty said. "Tell me the part about 'unity,' again?"

Ethel flushed and turned to Kevin. "I swear, Kevin, I didn't know. It was . . . she just said she was going to add some detergent to the face powder. I read online that it would make you itchy, give you a small rash. I had no idea it would cause anaphylactic shock!"

"People could have been seriously hurt!" I shouted, unable to contain myself. "People could have *died!*"

"I know!" she said, gulping back another sob. "Trust me, I know. It's over now. I promise you that."

"Oh, it's *definitely* over now," I said, my voice low. "*I* promise *you* that. I don't think you want to see what happens to you, if this doesn't end now."

"I get it. Of course." Ethel was meek now. Chastened. "And I want to make this up to you, if I can."

"Can you unswell Kevin's face?" Cheryl snapped. "Unterrorize my girlfriend and my best girl? Hardly."

"Okay, fair, but down, girl," I said, trying to calm the tensions rising in the room. "She can't undo what she did. But I'm sure there's some way that Ethel can try to make it right."

"Actually," Betty said, her eyes twinkling, "I have a perfect idea . . ."

CHAPTER TWENTY

> **Unknown Number:**
>
> See you at the Motorcade?

> **Evelyn:**
>
> Tonight? I'm busy, you know. I have to help prep the canapes.

> **Unknown Number:**
>
> Fine, sure. But you'll have a second to chat. After all, I know what you've been up to, and I know you're not THAT busy.

> **Evelyn:**
>
> Fine.

∿∿∿

JUGHEAD

It turned out, we had a *few* ideas of how Ethel could make up for her treachery and straight-up reckless endangerment of our friends.

The crux of our main plan? A good old-fashioned sting operation.

We'd set the trap collectively, and Ethel had dangled the bait. Evelyn really had no choice but to do what Ethel asked; when all was said and done, her partner kind of had a lot on her. And anyway, it wasn't some kind of crazy huge sacrifice for her to come to the Motorcade and Music. Ethel had told us Evelyn was being encouraged by Daddy Dearest to participate in all the Revels had to offer; thus, it didn't take much more than a few text exchanges to drag her to the Town Hall steps, right on cue.

It was six fifteen, and it felt like the entire town had gathered to hear Josie and Archie sing. In some ways, I couldn't help but be reminded of the last time we were all clustered together like this—*was it really only three days ago?*—quivering in collective anticipation: the time capsule. And we all knew how that had ended.

Hopefully, tonight would be less eventful. But considering what we had planned, it was hard to be entirely optimistic that we'd escape yet another festive occasion unscathed.

Betty, Veronica, Cheryl, Toni, and I were huddled by a maple tree closer to the street. This way, we could still watch our friends perform and hear the music, but we'd be a little more discretely located when Ethel came through with her end of the bargain. In the meantime, we were enjoying a small, momentary calm before the storm, swaying slightly, vaguely lost in the harmonic melodies coming from Archie and Josie.

I'd heard them perform together before, and they always sounded good—they were both so talented, after all—but there was something . . . I don't know, something *special* about their vibe tonight. They were in tune together—obviously, being as how they were musicians who were *literally* in tune with each other. But it was more than that . . . like being "in tune" on a whole other metaphorical level.

There was a kind of, I dunno, *peace* radiating from Archie as he strummed his guitar and leaned into his mic. The thing was, Archie hadn't had much peace since his trial. So none of this went unnoticed by yours truly.

I was kind of hoping, though, that it was going unnoticed by Veronica.

I mean, Archie *loves* Veronica with, like, a capital heart-eyed emoji. Of that, there was no doubt.

But there was also no denying the chemistry happening onstage.

Thankfully, we didn't have too much time to dwell on it. I heard footsteps from behind, and we all turned to find Ethel—and a very puzzled Evelyn—approaching.

When she spotted us, Evelyn came to an abrupt halt. Realization slowly dawned over her face, giving way to a look that was pinched and hardened with suspicion. Ethel gave her a shove, and Evelyn marched reluctantly over to our little group, even as her feet shuffled increasingly slowly. Ethel gave us a nod and headed in the other direction, having fulfilled her obligation.

"Come closer," Betty prompted. "We don't bite." She smiled sweetly.

"That is, we won't bite—if you have a good reason for having worked so hard to undo the Revels," Cheryl spat. "And endangering the life of my beloved."

Evelyn had the good graces to look appalled. "It was . . ." She looked around, searching for anyone who could rescue her from a Cheryl Blossom reckoning. But she was alone.

Good riddance.

"It was my dad," she started again. "He was hell-bent on us Farmies participating in the Revels. The pageant. Even though it all goes against everything the Farm teaches about authority and equality." Tears welled in her eyes, and next to me, Betty scoffed. "I guess . . ." She looked at Veronica. "Well, he said it was important to your mother that we cement our place in the community."

"Do *not* put this on my family," Veronica said. "You made a bad call. Own it."

"I . . ." Evelyn looked to be at a loss. She opened her mouth, then closed it again. Her eyes shone with tears. "Okay," she said finally. "I, uh, own it. I should have . . . I don't know, I should have pushed back, when my dad told me to get involved. I should have been honest with him about how I felt about the Revels. Feel."

Betty stepped forward, imposing, even in a pink suede moto jacket. "You could have. That's one idea," she agreed, voice low. "But you know, even if you weren't up for that? You still didn't have to straight up *sabotage* the pageant and hurt innocent people. You *know* that. What you did—what you *chose to do*—is sick and twisted. You could have just . . . turned the other cheek. I mean, isn't the Farm all about love and kindness? Community?"

Evelyn looked away.

"Maybe the pageant or the Revels or whatever went against the principals of the Farm. But don't tell me that sending Kevin Keller to the hospital didn't do that, too," Veronica said.

"You're right!" Evelyn said, breaking into loud, hiccupping sobs. "Of course you're right." She looked at Toni. "I'm sorry. I swear. I'm so sorry. You have to believe me."

"News flash, sister wife: She doesn't *have* to do anything," Cheryl snapped.

Evelyn's cheeks flamed red. "Of course."

"But I *do* believe you," Toni said, reaching out a reassuring arm. "And . . . I mean, I'm not going to say it was cool, obviously. But *we're* cool. I forgive you."

"You're just lucky my better half is so much more magnanimous than I am," Cheryl said, flipping her hair over her shoulder.

"I know," Evelyn said, sniffling. "I really do. And I appreciate it."

"Wait," Betty interrupted, fire still burning in her eyes as she spun around, looking at each of us in turn. "We're just forgiving her—just like that? After all she did? After all her *family's* done?"

"Betty," I said softly, and I tugged her sleeve gently, stepping a few feet away for some semblance of privacy in the midst of the crowd. "Evelyn isn't her father. And as much as I hate to admit it, this doesn't really seem to have anything to do with the Farm."

Betty opened her mouth to interrupt, but I continued. "I know everything that's going on with your mom and Polly has been hard, and it's not fair to you. None of it is. But remember, we promised that we were going to be methodical about this and not jump to any conclusions based on our personal feelings for the assortment of vile institutions in this town."

Betty took a deep breath and nodded slowly. "You're right, Jug. I just really thought—*hoped*—that it was all connected. That I finally had concrete proof that the Farm was as shady as it seems."

I pulled Betty in for a hug, tucking her against my chest. "We'll find it, Betts, I promise. But for right now, for this Revels mystery, it looks like we're back to square one."

Betty finally pulled away, and tightening her ponytail, she said, "Well, let's get back to it, then."

We rejoined the group, and Veronica and Betty appeared to have a quick, wordless conversation, at the end of which Veronica clapped her hands, taking charge.

"Okay, okay, well, it seems that all is forgiven—if not, I must say, immediately forgotten," Veronica said, shooting Evelyn a sharp look.

"But I think we can forget, later. As time goes on. A redemption arc is a gradual process." Veronica rubbed her hands together briskly now, leaning in to a topic change. "But let's put a pin in that—because here comes the motorcade."

I threw an arm across Betty's shoulder. "Gentlemen, start your engines," I murmured.

She glanced at me. "Gotta say, Juggie. If you'll pardon the pun—I'm still all revved up."

"I know," I said, kissing her on the top of her head, dodging her bouncing ponytail. "Miles to go, Betts."

FRIDAY

CHAPTER TWENTY-ONE

Reggie:

Yo, dawg—you and Josie sounded pretty good up there before the motorcade last night.

Archie:

Thanks, man.

Reggie:

Looked pretty, uh, hot and heavy too. Serious thirst vibes. ☺

Archie:

You're nuts, dude. I'm with Veronica.

Reggie:

If you say so. I'm just calling it like I see it . . .

ᔕᔕᔕ

CHERYL

Cocktails and Canapés—it was a hideous misnomer.

As a Blossom, I was accustomed to enjoying myself to the fullest at parties and other lavish extravaganzas, and had actually been quite looking forward to the well-hyped snacks at tonight's portion of the Revels. Did I trust the plebes of Riverdale's city offices to pull off a coup of unparalleled taste (no pun intended)? Of course not.

Still, though, at the barest of minimums, I had expected there would be *food*.

My stomach rumbled at the realization that, in fact, my expectations were apparently too high. Mind you, I'm accustomed to being let down by other people and their lesser visions.

"TeeTee," I said, turning to my radiant date for the night (and for all things in this world, if I have any say in the matter), "reports of canapés have been greatly exaggerated. I am bereft."

"I feel that," she agreed, scanning the room for a sign of anything even remotely edible. "We were gravely misled; I see exactly zero apps on the horizon." Considering the bar, she offered, "I could get us a couple of martinis and ask them to throw in a few extra olives?"

I laughed. "Cute. And ingenious as ever, my little scoundrel. But something tells me underaged drinking won't be easily condoned at an official Town Hall event. Hermione Lodge's own daughter may be an urban sophisticate with a notoriously checkered past, but even she seems to be teetotaling for just this one evening."

Toni raised an eyebrow toward Veronica, who was indeed carrying a rather chaste tumbler of what looked to be club soda with a twist and who raised it in our direction and made her way over to us, looking grateful for a refuge in this sea of over-dressed adults in ill-fitting off-the-rack.

"Ladies," she said, offering us both tiny air-kisses, "you both look smashing."

"Always," I agreed, pulling Toni closer and beaming. Attire for the event was meant to be "festive," but as usual, I'd chosen to pull out all the stops. I was in a custom cocktail-length dress in the deepest bloodred on the spectrum, trimmed with feathers at the hemline and beads at the plunging neckline. Antoinette was rocking a lace bustier minidress that was *tres* McQueen-meets-Serpent chic. Veronica herself, Riverdale's de facto First Daughter, was channeling an Ava Gardner–noir vibe with a slinky black halter and an amazing quartz cocktail ring that looked heavy enough to knock an untoward suitor's teeth out. "And likewise."

"Thanks," Veronica said, taking a sip from her drink. Her lipstick remained flawless, even as she left a deep gash of a waxy kiss on the lip of the glass. "Thank god for Marco, my stylist at Bendel, is all I'll say. If you're going to plan a multiday festival on an unsuspecting populace, you really need to give them enough notice to costume accordingly. And, you know, maybe recover from the trauma inherent in a Riverdale event in the first place."

"See, that's where I'm extra lucky." Toni grinned. "Not about the trauma, that is—though I'm healing. About the outfits. Cheryl's closet rivals any retailer."

"Ah, and surely, you must get special bae perks?" Veronica said, catching on.

"*Mais oui*, my beloved gets nothing less than an all-access pass," I confirmed.

I looked around. The Town Hall atrium was mostly full, the event in full swing, buzzing with the low hum of cocktail chatter: slow, muffled laughter, the occasional sharper exclamation. The clink of crystal on crystal, punctuated by a stiletto syncopation and the swoosh of more luxurious fabrics draping across skin. The air was heady with a mix of spicy floral perfumes, tangy aftershaves, and the astringent tinge of various unisex grooming products. Over it all, the sharply sweet echo of champagne laced the atmosphere, a cloud cover of its own. The greater populace seemed to be oblivious of the Revels-themed drama that had been occurring behind-the-scenes at Riverdale High.

"Speaking of baes, Veronica, where's yours?" I asked.

"Archie's on his way," she said. "He was helping his dad put the finishing touches on some of the setup for the block party."

"Such a little do-gooder, that orange Creamsicle–flavored confection of yours," I said, a twinkle in my eye.

She nodded, smiling to herself. "He is *definitely* the literal embodiment of 'stalwart.'"

"Ah, you must be talking about Archie now." Jughead swooped up, clutching a small plate of pigs in a blanket to his chest.

"Where did you get that?" I demanded.

He shrugged, grinning. "You just have to know who to talk to."

"I do," I told him. "You." I snatched one and devoured it before he had a chance to protest.

"My child. Such a healthy appetite." It was Mumsie, glaring down at me imperiously.

"Hello, Mother of the Damned," I sniped. "If you're here to drop loaded comments about my habits and appearance, you'll have to try again another day. I'm feeling far too fortified this evening."

"It's probably the mini hot dogs," Jughead said. "But actually, Mrs. Blossom, we were hoping to talk to you, Betty and I."

"Heavens, *why*?"

"We had a few questions, actually, Auntie," Betty said, slinking in her own perfectly girl-next-door cocktail apparel. "About the Revels. We were hoping that the Blossoms could shed some light on its history—considering your family's deep Riverdale roots."

Mumsie sniffed. "Well, naturally, our family has connections to the festival. We *are* one of Riverdale's founding families, as you know. Which means that we have a hand in helping to develop so many of the traditions that you now know and love." She smiled. "You saw with your own eyes; the time capsule barrel was one of Blossom Maple Farms' own."

The deadly calm with which she relayed this all was chilling. "Yes," Betty said, her voice catching slightly. "The barrel—with the body in it. Do you . . . do the Blossoms have any sense of who that might have been, in the time capsule? How they might have gotten inside there?"

"It was just a prank, my dear, you know that." Mumsie's eyes narrowed. "But I don't have to tell you that our family has known its fair share of struggles, its fair share of darkness." Her eyes welled up. "My own son, murdered by his weak, ineffectual father's hand!"

"There, there, kraken," I said. "Peddle your crocodile tears elsewhere."

"This town . . ." She looked at us. "This is a wicked town, with wicked desires. I should know. So, is it any wonder that something as joyful and celebratory as the Revels would ultimately be corrupted by blood?"

"No, not at all," Jughead said. "But we were thinking you might know something *specific*."

"It's sweet that you two lovebirds are so dedicated to uncovering truth and justice in our small, sordid town," she said, her voice low and lilting, dangerous. Was it a promise? A threat? A simple affect? Or all of the above? It was impossible to tell. Every inscrutable smile that crossed her face felt like a fortune cookie told in hieroglyphs, fraught with meaning that was impossible to decipher. "But the *truth* is just this: Our town, dark and wicked though it may be, is thriving."

"*Thriving?*" Jughead repeated, shaking his head. "Fizzle Rocks. Seizures. Dangerous games with deadly consequences."

She held her hands up. "My point is: This is what Riverdale *is*. What it has always been. This is our town's legacy. Rot and ruin . . . And our people? They *revel* in it. So why not let them?" She smiled, wistful. "It's so much easier than fighting it, swimming upstream."

"Maybe for you," Betty said, truly disturbed by what we were hearing, just as I was. "I still believe in Riverdale. I believe we can do better." It was what she had said at the Jubilee, two years ago, and it seemed that she meant it, *believed* in it, now more than ever.

Mumsie's expression turned tight. "Well," she said, suddenly brusque, "if I were you, I'd reconsider your course of action. I have no idea whose bones were found in the maple barrel, and I have no idea how they ended up there. But I suggest you find your friends, enjoy the Revels, and put all this ugliness aside. Because what you need to remember, children, is this: It doesn't *matter* who put that body in the maple barrel. There are plenty of people in this town who would do it, happily, if their tranquil existence was threatened.

"And there are *plenty* more maple barrels where that one came from."

A tiny buzzing sound came from her handbag, and she pulled her phone out and glanced at it. "Now, if you'll excuse me."

After she'd left, I exhaled a huge breath I hadn't realized I'd been holding.

"Is it just me, or did Penelope Blossom just low-key threaten to have us killed and stuffed in syrup barrels?" Jughead asked, incredulous.

"I don't think it's just you," I said. "And given how many people in our family have murdered *other* people in our family? I think you'd do well to take heed of her warning."

"I'm on board with that plan. But wait."

We all looked at Jughead. "What is it?" Betty asked him.

He pointed. "Pop Tate. All dapper and dressed up."

I looked. "Adorbs. And?"

"*And*, check out what he's wearing. Betty, look what he's *holding*. Think of the torn photo. The necklace and . . ."

Betty gasped. ". . . and the pocket watch."

"As fascinating as Pop's sartorial choices are," I said, cutting in, "I'm *so* over this. Can we please go find some freaking food?"

I turned on my heel, confident that anyone reasonable wouldn't be far behind me.

CHAPTER TWENTY-TWO

BETTY

Dear Diary:

Pop's pocket watch was some pretty telling evidence. But he was swarmed at the cocktail party, and no matter how hard we tried, Jughead and I couldn't snag a private moment with him. It was super frustrating, but we weren't going to let the rest of the night pass without any further investigation. Especially now that the Revels were drawing to a close.

"So what now, Jug?" I asked, feeling totally tapped out of brilliant ideas.

He shrugged, the expression on his face telling me he felt the exact same way that I did: lost, and confused. The pageant sabotage wasn't related to the body in the maple barrel, and nobody seemed to know anything about the old Revels—or if they did, they weren't talking. So when it came to the murder (or at least, what was feeling pretty likely to be murder), we were running out of leads.

One mystery solved, one to go. Why did it always work that way? Why didn't things ever tie up neat and tidy, like in the movies? I knew Jug had the same questions.

"I don't know," Jughead said. "But Penelope Blossom was being shady as ever. And the Blossoms <u>are</u> one of Riverdale's founding families. So, if we can't talk to Pop about the pocket watch…"

I finished his sentence for him. "Maybe we do another round of recon over at Thistlehouse. If there were ever a time to snoop around without being noticed, this is it."

"Snooping around? You definitely don't have to ask me twice," Jughead said, pulling his beanie down over his ears.

"I know." I smiled. "That's why I love you."

∿∿∿

Once we arrived, it took me about ten minutes to pick the lock to the front door with a bobby pin—an oldie but a goodie.

"It's like if MacGyver and Nancy Drew merged their genetics into the ultimate sleuth-slash-escape-artist," Jughead marveled.

I smiled at him and rolled my eyes, holding a finger up to my lips in the universal symbol for "shh."

"Okay," he stage-whispered. "But you know, we're actually alone here. Everyone in town was back at the cocktail party."

I shrugged. "Force of habit?"

We crept as softly as we could up the stairs to the second floor, and the various Thistlehouse bedrooms.

"Okay, so, we've got two leads in play, regarding a Blossom connection," Jughead was saying, turning to speak to me over his shoulder. "Besides the family's general history of nefariousness. One: The necklace from the torn photo we found at the library is the same design—if not the exact same necklace—as the one Nana Rose gave Polly.

"And two: The time capsule of death was actually a Blossom maple syrup barrel. Could be coincidence, I guess…but I think my feelings about coincidences have been made abundantly clear."

"Indeed," I said. "And I agree."

At the top of the stairs, we paused, gathering ourselves. "So if Polly said the necklace came from Nana Rose…" I started, slightly tentative.

"Then it stands to reason, we start in Nana Rose's room?" Jughead suggested.

"I think so? Who knows. Maybe we'll be lucky, and there'll be a jewelry box just sitting out in the open, with one of those damning crosses lying right inside." It was a fun fantasy, for a moment. But when was the last time luck played any kind of factor in Riverdale life?

"Start in Nana Rose's room for what, dear?"

I gasped and looked to see Nana Rose wheeling herself out of the bedroom, gazing at me with such intensity I immediately felt uncomfortable. Her skin was powdery, translucent, and thin like onion paper. I could see a road map of blue veins tracing a lacy, snaking pattern across her temples, where her pulse beat lightly.

She looked fragile, yes—every bit her age—but she somehow looked steely, too. Like a person who knew things, dreadful things—but some-how wasn't afraid of <u>anything</u>.

"Nana Rose—what are you doing here?" I faltered.

She laughed. "I could ask the same of _you_, dearie. I have missed your visits. Of course, I understand. It must be hard for you. Since we lost Jason."

Jughead glanced at me, his meaning clear: _She thinks you're Polly._ It had happened before. He tried to suppress a telling smile: That probably made this whole thing a lot easier.

"It's been a while," I said, feeling guilty for misleading an old woman but unable to take the chance that was being offered up on a silver platter. "I'm so sorry. I've missed you. But"—I said, in a burst of inspiration—"I've been wearing the cross you gave me."

A warm smile crept across her face. "The cross! How delightful. Oh, I'm so glad to hear that. The design has been in our family for generations. We give that particular charm to all our Blossom daughters on the eve of their confirmation."

"So there's more than one?" My heart sank. That definitely lowered our clue's stock value, even if only slightly. There was no telling which Blossom's necklace was the one from the newspaper article. Were we at another dead end?

"Oh, don't you worry; you're still one of a kind, Polly. And what have you been up to, lately?"

We'd wanted a chance to ask someone about the Blossoms' history with the Revels. But then again—Nana Rose thought I was Polly. Was she even fully lucid right now?

I had no idea. The only thing I _did_ know with any certainty was that I didn't want to have had come out to Thistlehouse, to get this close to a break, only to turn back because I'd been spooked by a slightly batty old lady.

I looked at Jug, and, together, we decided: It was worth a try. She was <u>right here</u>. We probably wouldn't get another chance like this one.

"I, uh…well, we've been busy at the Farm, of course. And"—it was now or never—"preparing for the Revels."

Her face darkened. "The <u>Revels</u>," she spat. "An abomination on this abominable town. It should have stayed an ugly footnote in history, where it belonged."

"But why?" Jughead couldn't help himself; he rushed to Nana Rose's side. "It was a celebration. For a long time. But it's <u>not</u> in the town historical record. Why does no one want to talk about its history? Why aren't there any articles about it in any of the Riverdale papers? The only thing we could find—barely—was a piece on the Miss Maple pageant. A piece that had been destroyed."

"Well, good riddance to <u>that</u>," she huffed.

"Nana Rose, why do people want to act like the original Revels—all of it—never happened?" I asked, trying to keep my voice even.

"Because the original Revels were an atrocity!" Nana Rose shouted, suddenly vehement and filled with rage. "And that pageant you speak of? It was built on a river of blood and a bed of bones."

A chill ran down my spine. We were so close. I thought of the skull tumbling from the maple barrel, that long, straggly hair entwined with earthworms, maggots…all the creatures that slither in the dirt. "What does that mean? Whose blood? Whose bones?"

Maybe Nana Rose was <u>exactly</u> the person we needed to be speaking with. Maybe the truth was that only someone semi-lucid would be able to relay something truly horrific to us.

She gave a deep sigh. "As you know, child, Riverdale was founded seventy-five years ago. But the settlers who built this town arrived much earlier than that."

"Early 1700s," Jughead said. "That was what Weatherbee told us."

"Yes," she agreed, "1701, or thereabouts. It was a different era. Primitive. Savage. People had…funny superstitions. Even <u>our</u> people."

"Meaning, the Blossoms?" I guessed.

She nodded. "The original Grandpappy Blossom first came to the banks of Sweetwater River to make his trade in maple syrup. He struggled, at first, but after his first bountiful harvest, he and the other settlers celebrated."

"The original Riverdale Revels," I said, recalling Weatherbee's speech at the school assembly.

She nodded again, shorter this time. "It was 1706. The settlers were so grateful, they decided to…well, they felt they had to do something. So they chose to devise a ceremony. To appease the higher powers going forward, to ensure that the taps wouldn't run dry, ever again."

"Nana Rose, what was the ceremony?" I asked, dread forming a block of ice in my belly. I doubted it was something great and harmless. Unwittingly, I clenched my hands so tightly I felt an immediate stinging in my palms from where my fingernails had broken the skin.

"Like I say, our forefathers were…a superstitious group. They thought what might be needed was…a sacrifice."

I clapped my hands over my mouth in horror, tears springing to my eyes. "<u>A sacrifice?</u>" I echoed, unable to believe the words coming out of my mouth.

"To appease the powers that be, just as I told you," she said. She was short, matter-of-fact.

"Let me guess," Jughead said. "They'd find the prettiest virgin in town?" He exhaled, long. "Fun times."

"They held a…contest of sorts."

I could barely breathe. "Like a pageant."

"Well, you could call it that, dearie. Of a sort, in any case. A small group of local girls would be gathered, rounded up every few years. The elder settlers—they would be considered the town council, I suppose, in modern times—would select one of the young women—the most innocent, most pure of heart, yes. She would be their tribute. It was considered a great honor."

My stomach seized. "A great honor?" I repeated slowly. "To be murdered and crammed into a maple barrel?"

"Maple barrel? Where are you getting that from, sweet Polly? No, these girls were hanged. From that large maple, the resplendent one just in the center of the clearing beyond Fox Forest. After the hanging, they'd be buried beneath the tree."

I knew the tree she was talking about. It was stunning: towering higher and thicker than any other around for miles. I felt queasy, thinking about what it had been thriving on for so many years. My vision tunneled, and the room went dark. Blood rushed to my ears.

A young girl...every few years. Sentenced to her death, and hung from a tree in Fox Forest? _How many...?_

It was more gruesome than I could ever have imagined. "Sacrifice?" I echoed, numb. She nodded.

"How?" Jughead asked when he could manage to speak again. "I mean, we're talking about...something like, what? Fifty girls, over the years. Just vanished. So how was this happening and no one in the town was doing anything to stop it? How did no one notice?"

Nana Rose regarded him with frank curiosity. "Notice? They all _noticed_, of course. You seem to be missing one simple fact: _They were all a part of it._ All our citizens, all our neighbors. There was nothing to stop, you see."

"But..." I was still struggling to put the pieces together. "These girls, these"—I choked the word out—"_these sacrifices_...they had families, people who cared about them. Someone in their lives who would notice they were..." I trailed off, already knowing where this was going, what her answer would be.

"Child," she said, softly chiding me, "you come from a world of ViewTube and SpaceTime. You can't imagine how different it was then. When the Revels first started, it was an easy enough plan to execute, with the whole of the town complicit. Witch trials had mostly subsided by the 1700s, of course, but they weren't completely gone from consciousness. And it was believed that there were several covens settled nearby, hiding in plain sight, so to speak. In the area we know today as Greendale. It was easy enough to vilify young women."

"The more things change…" Jughead muttered.

But I didn't have time for that now. "So the girls…" I said, pushing.

"Ah, yes. Our ancestors had help there. It was a nunnery, one which bore only the faintest resemblance to the one you knew."

"The Sisters of Quiet Mercy," I breathed.

"Yes, although they hadn't yet adopted that name for their church at the time. They found orphans, girls who had slipped through the cracks. Girls who wouldn't be missed. Devout girls, even amid a time of dark arts and alleged witchcraft."

"<u>Nuns</u>. Fed the town <u>human sacrifices</u>?" Jughead asked.

She gave a small shrug. "As time went on, it did become more of a challenge to keep the girls aligned with the town's vision."

"I'll bet," Jughead said.

"It was the Blossoms who kept their doors open with our financial generosity—which in turn led to a more amenable attitude on their part."

"When did it stop?" I asked.

"The practice was abolished right before the Civil War, with the arrival of a so-called progressive mayor—though he wouldn't have been called mayor then. Theodosius Little. Surely you learned about him in civics class?"

"What?" I was delirious. "Oh, uh, yes." Hazy details floated in the back of my mind, slippery as fish. I dimly recalled one specific point, from the photo we'd seen at Pop's earlier in the week, back when the Revels had first been announced. That felt like ages, a lifetime, ago now. My head spun just thinking about everything that had happened since that day. "His family and the Tate family were old friends, right?

"Yes, that's the one. It was his initiative, to put an end to the 'revelry,' but by all accounts, he didn't meet much resistance. Most felt it was about time. The revels were replaced by an actual pageant and a simpler, happier festival. To keep the tradition of celebrating our harvest alive."

"Wait," Jughead said, his eyes sparkling as he thought it through. "The <u>Miss Maple pageant</u> was actually a reboot of a tradition of <u>virgin sacrifice</u>?"

"Exactly, dearie. A revival, as my generation would say." She gave a coy, girlish smile, endearing even though it was at odds with her whole general countenance.

Jughead pulled off his beanie and ran his fingers through his hair, looking manic and totally taken aback. "Veronica <u>really</u> wasn't wrong about the misogynistic undertones of this event," he muttered, more to himself than anyone else.

"But..." I was still struggling to put the pieces of this utterly insane story together. "The new festival, and the pageant, too. That was completely excised from all the local history books, erased. Why?"

"Hmm." Nana Rose squinted, concentrating. "Oh yes! The Revels were abolished in 1941, along with the Miss Maple pageant, when the town was officially founded. Another one of those so-called modern mayors—he didn't want <u>any</u> reminder of our town's sordid past. That's what the time capsule was for—to bury the past, metaphorically speaking. Although it seems someone did take it literally." Nana Rose giggled, a sound that was totally jarring within the context of our horrifying conversation.

"And they left it for others to puzzle out, seventy-five years later. That is some hard-core passing of the buck," Jughead said.

"Many were opposed to abolishing the pageant," Nana Rose explained. "The time capsule was a bone to throw—that if we were ending the tradition, we would go out on a bit of a bang, you know. Leave a legacy for future generations."

I exhaled. "Well, that you definitely did."

"Clearly the Revels have always been fraught with great controversy. Not even our family could escape its toxic reach." She peered at me, the milky blue of her cataract-covered eyes so laser sharp I felt myself taking a step back from her.

"I myself never had the chance to compete in the pageant," she said, sounding mournful at the thought. "But it was the source of an enormous conflict for my cousins Adelaide and Emmaline Blossom. They were twins, great beauties. Both considered top contenders to win the crown. Then Emmaline had a…tryst with a traveling salesman. When it was discovered, her reputation was irrevocably tarnished." Nana Rose looked down, clearly shaken by the memory. "The two sisters quarreled, and Adelaide turned on Emmaline. She was run out of town. The two sisters never repaired that rift. It was tragic."

"It's a sad story," Jughead agreed. "Did they wear matching cross necklaces, too? Like the one you gave Polly?"

Nana Rose smiled. "Indeed."

"I thought so," Jughead said, satisfied. "Still, it's only slightly <u>less</u> sad than the story about all those girls who were straight-up hung to appease the gods of the maple trees."

Nana Rose looked at him, taken aback. "Well, but, sonny," she said, as if explaining something to a very small, very simple child, "Adelaide and Emmaline were <u>family</u>."

SATURDAY

CHAPTER TWENTY-THREE

Betty:

So much to fill you guys in on! You were gone by the time Jug and I came down from talking to Nana Rose!

Veronica:

Sorry, Archie got a text from his dad and needed to meet him. Details, please?

Betty:

In person—it's too much for a text. Please prepare to have your mind blown.

Veronica:

Not totally sure how to prepare for that, but I'll do what I can.

∿∿∿

ARCHIE

"Tell me you didn't know about this."

My father looked up from where he was hanging a sign for Pop's hamburger-eating contest that afternoon. He looked surprised to see me. More likely, it was the fact that Betty, Veronica, Jug, and I were standing over him, totally stunned and looking for answers.

"Arch? You're early. Or are you here to tell me you can't help your old man out with this anymore?"

"What? No. I mean—yeah, of course I'll help, Dad. But first—*we need to talk.*"

He stopped hammering and really looked at me, like he was maybe finally taking in the expression on my face. On all our faces. "You know," he said after a minute, "I've been at this for a while now and I'm starving. The burger-eating contest isn't until later. How about we grab some hot dogs and I take a break, and you can ask me all about . . . whatever this is."

ᴧᴧᴧ

Twenty minutes later, we were hunkered down on the steps of the Main Street Snip 'N Shear. Betty and Jughead had told Veronica and me all about the Revels history—human sacrifices and all—and we had to know how much our parents knew, and why they had kept it from us.

"Did you know?" I asked again, once Jughead had finished giving him the full breakdown.

Dad sighed and ran his hand over his hair. "*No*, of course not! Son, I'm not going to lie to you. I had heard stories, you know, about the Maple Man. But to me, he was always . . . just a boogeyman. A cautionary tale you'd tell children. You know, the Maple Man will snatch you if you misbehave, bury you beneath a maple tree. If I had *any* idea it was rooted in truth . . . son, you can bet I would have warned you. *Protected* you."

"I believe you," I said, meaning it. But still, it wasn't totally enough.

"Charming," Jughead said, furrowing his brow. The explanation obviously wasn't enough for him, either. "A children's story, you say? The Brothers Grimm's finest might have been more upbeat."

"Every town has its version of that," Fred said. "When I was a kid, of course, I believed it. But once I got older, I just recognized it for the urban legend that it is."

"But it wasn't," Betty said, urgency in her voice. "Well, I mean, your version was, of course, but it was based on something horrific that was *really happening*. And no one ever talks about it."

"Betty," I pointed out, understanding how frustrated she

was feeling, "they legit *didn't know.* I mean, if Nana Rose was telling the truth—I mean, if she remembers it right, and stuff—"

"She does," Betty swore, shaking her head insistently. "She thought I was Polly, fine, but about the important things? The big things? She's always in her right mind about those."

"I don't know if I'd go so far as, *always* . . . But she . . . sounded pretty convincing, Arch," Jughead said. "I was there. Betty's right."

"But my dad didn't know. None of your parents probably did, either. It was an *urban legend.*"

"Frankly, I think I preferred blissful ignorance," my dad added.

"You and everyone else in this town," Betty said, distraught. "Did I tell you how my own mother had zero interest in investigating the body in the maple barrel? She's a *news reporter,* and this is a possible *murder,* and not only did she not want to look into it herself, she full-on got *mad* at me when I tried to ask her about it."

Dad looked at Betty. His expression got soft as he considered her. "Here's the thing, Betty," he said, putting a hand on her shoulder. "Anyone who's grown up in this town? We've seen its darkness. We've known it our whole lives. And if a tradition was around for a hundred-odd years and then—poof—stopped in its tracks? Well, those of us who paid attention in local history lessons knew not to ask questions. We knew there was probably a reason it stopped, and it was probably a reason we didn't want to know. I'm sure your mom heard the same urban legends I did—and if she was anything like me, she didn't want to think too hard about the real-life inspiration behind the legend."

He gave her shoulder a squeeze. "Lord knows, your mom isn't perfect—let me be the first to say that—but, Betty, she's human. She makes mistakes. At the end of the day, she loves you. Give her a break for not wanting to do a deep dive on yet another skeleton in Riverdale's closet."

"She told you she was busy with the Farm," Jughead reminded her. "And that doesn't seem to be a lie or even an exaggeration. It's entirely possible that this was just a case of her choosing to ignore whatever normal alarm bell might go off in her investigative reporter brain, in the interest of something she thought was more important."

"That would explain my mother's behavior, too," Veronica added. "As mayor, she's presided over some truly horrific moments in Riverdale's living history. She'd want the win, and if she learned something atrocious, the hard way, by opening Pandora's box—"

"More like Pandora's time capsule," Jughead quipped.

"*However* you want to dub it," Veronica continued, "I could see her thinking a million-year-old blip on the radar wasn't worth upending her grand plan to rebuild our town's spirits. In

Riverdale, the old mantra 'no publicity is bad publicity' doesn't really hold up."

"One thing still doesn't make sense, though," Betty protested.

"*One* thing?" Jughead laughed.

Betty gave him a small smile. "When we were at Pop's that day—when your father was talking to us about opening the time capsule. He said that there were some people who'd really pushed to bring the Revels back. But neither of them said anything more."

"I remember," Jughead said. "Pop was pretty quiet. Which— he gets that way, but . . ."

"But," I agreed.

"Well, it's not like you won't have a chance to see him, to ask him a few questions," Veronica pointed out. "He's got hundreds of burgers to cook before the contest this afternoon."

"It feels weird, though," Betty said. "Celebrating the Revels at all, I mean now that we know its ghoulish history. All those girls who *died*. And everyone—the whole town—they just went along with it. For more than a century." She shivered, even though it wasn't that cold out, and she was wearing a jacket.

"I hear you, Betty," my dad said. "But Riverdale's skeletons will be locked in the town's proverbial closets whether you celebrate the revived Revels or not. You can't change the past. You can only impact the future—by reclaiming the Revels and giving them a purely positive meaning for our town. For our history—going forward."

"I think 'history going forward' is an oxymoron," Jughead said, "but I get what you're saying, Mr. Andrews, and I'll allow it. It's a good point. *We* can turn the bad memory into something good."

"It's all that we can do," Dad said.

CHAPTER TWENTY-FOUR

BETTY

Dear Diary:

In the end, it was actually almost straightforward—in a twisted sort of way, of course. Jughead and I should have realized it, the second we talked to Nana Rose about the history of the Revels. But of course, given the horror of what she was revealing to us, we were more than a little bit preoccupied.

Once it clicked, though, I was convinced that talking to Pop Tate would be the final key to understanding the connection between the body in the maple barrel and the sordid history of the Revels. He had the pocket watch, and he had the family connection to the mayor, to the Revels. He had to be the missing link here.

All around us the block party was in full swing: booths selling smoothies, Reggie's dad's top collectible cars on display since the Motorcade finished, a WRIV tent handing out bumper stickers as Mom grabbed random passersby for Revels-related sound bites. But Archie, Jughead, Veronica, and I were single-minded, fixated on Pop Tate, and what he might have known about the Riverdale Revels' dark origins. He was easy enough to pin down—we found him manning the grill at his booth.

"You kids here for the burger-eating contest?" Pop asked, his eyes twinkling.

"Sadly, no," Jughead said. "Actually, we really need to talk to you."

"To me?" He looked surprised. "About what?"

"Pop, we know you know about the Revels—the _original_ Revels," Veronica said seriously.

His expression darkened. "I don't know what you're talking about."

"We know, too. About the history, the sacrifices." I fixed him with a steady gaze. "_You know_. And I'm willing to bet you know the truth about the time capsule, too."

"Betty, what are you going on about?" Pop asked. He was trying to sound light—but he was trying too hard. I could see it in the worried glint in his eye.

"Pop, it's okay. I understand why you wanted to hide the town's history from us. But the fact that our ancestors sacrificed pure young women as part of their Riverdale Revels still doesn't explain how _a skeleton_ ended up in a maple barrel time capsule more than seventy-five years later. And we need answers."

"And you think I have them?"

"Nana Rose told us about your family's connection to the first mayor of Riverdale," Jughead said.

"And how Mayor Little abolished the original Revels in 1861," I continued.

"Didn't you say that your family had been close with the Little family, going way back?" Archie asked, not really expecting an answer.

Jughead peered at Pop, intent. "We know that in 1941, when the murder-free Revels were canceled for good, the town created a time capsule. I'm guessing the dead body inside wasn't on the original agenda."

"Pop, there was a photo," I said. "From an article—the only article—about Miss Maple. It was damaged, but it was a picture of a cross...and, I think, that pocket watch you were wearing last night."

I swallowed, then looked at him. "Your family goes almost as far back as the Blossoms around here. And someone in your family was involved with at least one of those pageants, front and center enough to have made it into a picture in the news. So if you know anything... please...tell us."

Pop paused for a moment, breathing hard. He was obviously considering what to tell us, how much. "Pop," Veronica implored, "it's over. Just...give us the truth."

He took a deep sigh. "You kids want the truth? It's an ugly one, at that. But then, you know that, given everything you've lived through here, in this town."

We all nodded, solemn, listening.

"You know the story behind the Revels. Young girls being murdered, strung up in Fox Forest. Eventually, the practice died out, thank the good lord. But my ancestors, they knew eventually the day would come—that someone with enough power would come along and erase the whole bloody history of the festival. And they couldn't let that happen."

"Those who forget history are doomed to repeat it," Jughead said, nodding. Pop made a noise of agreement.

"So the year that the time capsule was to be buried—the year the door was officially closing on the Revels forever, my grandfather and his brother, they waited until dark…and they dug one of the poor girls up."

We all gasped in unison. This story had just transcended into a new level of horror show.

"They pulled her out. They broke the seal on the time capsule, and they laid her to rest inside. When it was buried a few days later, no one was any the wiser. And there her bones have stayed ever since.

"When my dad got a little older, his father told him what he had done back during the founding. And then later my daddy told me. Generations of Tates have passed along our legacy: custodians of this knowledge, of the Maple Woman."

Jughead was still slowly processing. "So the time capsule was…"

"I suppose you could call it a precautionary measure," Pop said slowly. "A lot can change in seventy-five years. People grow older, they forget. Grandpa Tate knew eventually the Revels would be resurrected. He wanted to be sure that the people of Riverdale remembered their <u>real</u> history. That way, when the capsule was opened generations later…"

"Cat's out of the bag." Archie shuddered. "And we'd all have to face the truth."

"At the Jubilee," Jughead said. "That was when this all was supposed to happen."

"Yes. But things were so...it was a dark time, with the Blossom boy being killed," Pop said, his face creased in pain. "The town council canceled their plans for the Revels—and the time capsule. All I could do was wait for the right moment to suggest it was time to bring the Revels back—and let everything play out the way Grandpa Tate intended."

"And no one had any idea..." I said.

"...because basically every single news article or record about it had been destroyed," Jughead finished.

"Exactly." He sighed. "But in time, it became clear enough that there wasn't going to be a 'right time' to bring the truth to light. Something dark always seemed to be brewing." His eyes shone. "That's the nature of evil."

"So now what?" Archie asked.

"Now the truth finally comes to light," I said, resolute. "Even if people in this town don't want to face it."

"B," Veronica placed a hand on my arm. "You know I've got your back, ride-or-die. But..."

"But?" I looked at her. Where was she going with this?

"What if...the truth didn't come to light?" She glanced around at our puzzled faces.

"We...bury the truth." I turned the idea over in my head.

"Who's it going to help at this point, anyway?" Veronica said softly. "This town…hasn't it seen enough death? My mother brought the Revels back—"

"—because Pop talked her into it," Jughead interjected.

"Well, okay, but, whatever my mom's faults are—and I think we can agree, I'm pretty straight about her having <u>plenty</u>—she legit wanted the Revels to be something nice for this town. Something to unify us, amid…all the darkness."

<u>All the darkness.</u>

I thought about my father, rotting in a prison cell. I thought about my mother, too caught up in a creepy cult to be even marginally aware of the craziest murder story this town had seen in two hundred years (which was, in and of itself, saying a lot). I thought about the semipermanent marks I had in my fists from clenching my hands so tightly against exactly that darkness, for so long.

"Bury it," I mused.

"Exactly," she said. "So many of our friends worked so hard for the Revels and this pageant, and they're really looking forward to it. The whole town is, really."

"Burying it—at least that's on theme," Jughead said.

"I can't believe you're pushing for the pageant, V," I said, laughing a little. "You were totally opposed to it when your mom first made the announcement."

"Oh, I remember," she said, smiling to herself. "But I think Pop is onto something. This town knows <u>more</u> than enough darkness. We deserve to take a beat and pave the way for something brighter."

"Okay," I said slowly. "We bury it."

"We cover it up," Jughead said. "For the town's sake. But we don't forget."

We all nodded, and I saw a wave of calm come over Pop Tate's face for the first time in who knows how long. I knew none of us could have forgotten the truth, even if we'd tried.

"For now," Veronica said, prodding us out of our collective reverie, "let's get going. We have a pageant to get to."

EPILOGUE

JUGHEAD

Backstage at the Riverdale High auditorium, tension was thick enough to spread on a pancake. After Evelyn and Ethel's confession, the antics and incidents that had plagued earlier rehearsals had stopped. Now people were purely excited to be competing. But no amount of preparation would ever truly feel like enough. Your intrepid boy reporter may have chosen to abstain from the festivities, but I observed, with my keen writer's eye, as contestants like Fangs Fogarty and Peaches 'N Cream went through last-minute changes to their interview responses, tuned instruments for talent portions, ran through vocal warm-ups, stretches, and slathered—was that really *Vaseline*? Yes, it was—on their teeth. I saw Cheryl wave a lint brush over Toni as Toni teetered in impossibly tall heels and even taller hair. Kevin, too, was in the wings, his swelling having mostly gone down, and whatever residual might have been left, more than dwarfed by the broad smile on his face. My own leading lady, Betty, stood with her best friend, taking selfie after selfie from behind the scenes, laughing in between each click of the phone's camera.

The feeling of competition was thick. But so was the sense of joy. Of promise. And we all were going to bask in it. We'd each of us spent more than our share of time in the darkness.

Pop was right, we knew. And so was Mr. Andrews. The town deserved the truth, but our friends?

They deserved this moment to shine.

Reggie Mantle straightened the bow tie on his tuxedo. He smiled his heartthrob smile. Surveying the group of eager, assembled students, he clapped his hands. He exchanged a look with Cheryl, the eager Mistress of Ceremonies for the evening, received her nod of acknowledgement smoothly.

"Places, everyone," he called. "It's about that time."

ABOUT THE AUTHOR

© JDZ Photography

Micol Ostow has written over fifty works for readers of all ages, including projects based on properties like *Buffy the Vampire Slayer*, *Charmed*, and, most recently, *Mean Girls: A Novel*. As a child, she drew her own Archie Comics panels, and in her former life as an editor, she published the *Betty & Veronica Mad Libs* game. She lives in Brooklyn with her husband and two daughters, who are also way too pop culture–obsessed. Visit her online at micolostow.com.